Study guide for
Order of Eastern Star

Prepared by PGM Myra Williams

 Be mindful:

This study guide is comprised of things I have collected or made over the years by other Eastern Star members or myself. This is just a study guide.

Table of contents

Dedication

This study guide is dedicated to every member of The Order of Eastern Star (OES). The amazing journey in the organization is mind blowing and I have met some awesome people and continuing to meet some amazing people. The organization is built on the foundation of helping our community alongside our Masonic brothers.

Acknowledgement

I would like to take this time to give acknowledgement to Past Grand Matron Kapre McKinney for being my study buddy for many years and Sister Michelle Davis for bringing old stuff and making it fresh. Past Grand Master Ron Foster for having the undying faith in me to help you lead the Dig Deeper forum. To Past Grand Matron Arthurretta Ivory for always challenging me. I could have never been the person I am today in this organization without you. I would like to thank my loving parents (Lester and Georgia Williams) and sister (Sister Michelle Williams) for believing in me and finally my amazing chapter Ladies of Jasmine #26 of Houston, Tx I love you ladies."

About the Author

My Name is PGM Myra Williams have been an Eastern Star for

21 years. I joined the Order in 2001 under RoseMary Grand Chapter and

Abraham Grand Lodge A.F. & A.M. I am a pillar of the Eastern Star Community.

Teaching what I have learned and what I know as a member of OES. I have obtained my higher

House degrees in the Order (Queen of the South, Amaranth, Heroines of Jericho, Lady Knights and Daughter of the Sphinx).

I am now a Past Grand Matron with an abundance of knowledge and co-owner

of Dig Deeper education.

These days you can find me teaching others about the order.

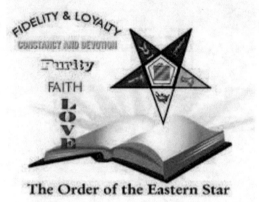

The Order of the Eastern Star

Introduction to the Order of Eastern Star

Welcome to the Order of the Eastern Star!

You are now a member of the largest fraternal organization in the world for both men and women. Its members are composed of men who are Master Masons and women with specific relationships to Master Masons.

Though its teachings are based on the Bible, the Order of the Eastern Star espouses no religion and is neither secret or political.

To better understand the Order, you should always study with following:

- Your ritual
- Your Bible (at least 2 different versions; one being King James Version)
- Your study materials you are given

There is a lot of information to learn. Do not get discouraged if you cannot learn it all in one sitting. That is what study sessions and other sisters are for; stay focused, and strive to emulate the five Heroines that this order is based on.

WHAT IS THE
ORDER OF THE EASTERN STAR

Someone may ask no matter who you are
What is the Order of the Eastern Star?
If you've not been a member for a while or so,
There are just a few facts you may want to know.
We belong to an Order, the largest of its kind.
A fraternity in which men and women you will find.
Its members are found in every corner of the glove,
And each is part of the great Masonic fold.
Our purpose is to inspire good; its that simple and plain;
The tenets of truth, charity, loyalty and kindness we train.
Charitable and benevolent projects are the things we do
To help friends in need and to see their trouble through.
Our principals are based on Biblical days
But in no way conflict with our religious ways.
We have lots of fun, too, as everyone should,
Meeting and traveling and working for good.
And because of our goals, we develop a bond
For each member, one to another, we become very fond.
This is an Order like no other you will find,
A chance to do good for your fellow mankind.
-Author Unknown-

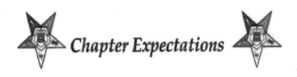 # Chapter Expectations

 Faithfulness of the Obligation

 Strict Devotion of the Eastern Star Landmarks

 Conduct yourself with Integrity and in a manner that is conductive to being a "Woman of God"

 Willingness to S.E.R.V.E. God's people

 Cooperation, Attendance and 100% participation

 Most importantly be loyal and respectful to your sisters and The Order

DRESS CODE

SISTERS

- White nursing uniforms with long sleeves or ¾ length sleeves with full regalia will be worn during initiations, conferring of degrees, for all Grand Chapter/Grand Lodge events (i.e. Palm Sunday, OES Weekend Church service, St. John's Day church service, and Grand Supreme).
- Casual dress will be worn during all monthly business meetings
- Casual dress consists of Chapter button down and black skirt.
- Skirts should fall below the knees when seated
- No see through skirts should be worn
- Pantyhose should be worn, no knee highs or thigh highs
- Shoes must be closed in, both heel and toe
- White close-toe pumps or nursing shoes are to be worn with nursing uniforms
- Pants are never to be worn at any time during a business meeting
- Regalia (fez, member pin, gloves, sash and scarf) must be worn to Grand functions and any meeting where elections are held and degrees will be conferred

BROTHERS

- Aprons must be worn at all meeting
- Casual dress will be worn during all monthly business meetings
- Black suit with white shirt and black ties are standard uniform when election are held and degrees will be conferred
- Black shoes and socks
- Collars must be worn in addition to aprons when degrees will be conferred
- Casual dress consists of chapter shirts and black slacks

THE LANDMARKS

1. The Eastern Star is the basis of the Five Degrees of the Adoptive Rite; the name and character of the Rite are unchangeable.
2. Its lessons are Scriptural; its teachings are moral; and its purposes are beneficent.
3. Its obligations are based upon the honor of the female sex who obtain its ceremonies, and are framed upon the principle that whatever benefits are due by the Masonic Fraternity to the wives, widows, daughters and sisters of Masons; corresponding benefits are due from them to the Brotherhood.
4. Each candidate shall declare a belief in the existence of a Supreme Being, who will, sooner or later, punish the willful violation of solemn pledge.
5. The modes of recognition, which are the peculiar secrets of the Rite, cannot, without destroying the foundation of the system, be changed.
6. A covenant of secrecy voluntarily assumed is perpetual from the force of such obligation there is no possibility of release.
7. The control of the Rite lies in the State Grand Chapter of the Adoptive Rite.
8. The ballot for candidates for membership must be unanimous, and is to be kept inviolably secret.
9. It is the right of every Chapter to be the judge of who shall be admitted to its membership, and to select its own officers, but in no case can the ceremonies of the Order be conferred unless a Master Mason in good standing in the Masonic Fraternity presides.
10. Every member is amenable to the laws and regulations of the Order, and may be tired for offenses, though he or she may permanently or temporarily reside within the jurisdiction of another Chapter.
11. It is the right of every member to appeal from the decision of a Subordinate Chapter to the Grand Chapter of the State.
12. It is the prerogative of the Grand Patron to preside over every assembly of the Rite wherever he may visit, and to grant Dispensations for the formation of new Chapters in the State.
13. Every Chapter has the right to dispense the light of the Adoptive Rite and to administer its own private affairs.
14. Every Chapter should elect and install its officers annually.
15. Every member may visit and sit in every regular Chapter, except when such visitor is likely to disturb the harmony or interrupt the progress of the Chapter he or she proposes to visit.

The Obligation

You will carefully preserve in sacred and inviolable secrecy, and under no circumstances improperly divulge any of the ceremonies, signs or passes belonging to the Order of the Eastern Star.

You will cheerfully obey the constitution and all the rules and regulations of the Supreme Grand Chapter and the by-laws of the chapter of which you may be a member.

You will, so far as in your power, liberally dispense to your sisters advice in their troubles, sympathy in their sorrows, and aid in their misfortunes.

You will cautiously avoid speaking evil of your sisters, or performing any acts of injustice or unkindness toward them.

_____

Signature/Date

NEED TO KNOW INFORMATION

ENTERING AND LEAVING A CHAPTER MEETING WHILE IN SESSION

To leave a Chapter Meeting while in session, place your purse and/or other items down in the West or on the sideline, proceed to a position in front of the Associate Matron and Associate Patron and give the Salutation Sign and wait on the Associate Matron's response. If entering late, approach the altar between Esther and Martha and holding your hands in the sign of salutation (honors) and wait for the Worthy Matron's response. If retiring, give appropriate salutation to the East and West, approach the Associate Matron and wait for the Warder to open the door to the Chapter Room. If ill or in it is an emergency, you may leave the Chapter Room through the preparation room door without giving the Salutation Sign.

CONDUCTING CHAPTER BUSINESS

Any organization has a certain amount of business that must be transacted. The Chapter will use Roberts Rule of Order as guide for conducting the business of the meeting. Participate in the business of the Chapter by asking questions or requesting clarification on any point, which is not clear to you. Raise your right hand slightly higher than your head, wait until acknowledged, stand up and say "Worth Matron...." Make motions by saying "Worthy Matron, I (state position and name) move that ..." Voting is done "by the usual sign of the Order," which is the raising of the right hand. Direct all conversation to the East.

WHAT THE GAVEL RAPS MEAN

The Presiding officer who is usually the Worthy Matron is responsible for the use of the Gavel. *raps of the Gavel calls sup the entire Chapter to a standing position, * raps calls up the elected officers and *rap calls the Chapter to order, * rap seats Chapter when standing, *rap complete the Opening and Closing Ceremonies and * rap completes any order of business or voting.

HONORS SIGN

Give the Grand Honors in one motion by crossing the arms over the breast, the *over the *, with hands open with a slight bow. Grand Honors are given to Worthy Grand Matrons, Worthy Grand Patrons, Past Grand Matrons and Past Grand Patrons, the Deputy Grand Master and the Grand Master.

Subordinate Chapter honors are given to the Worthy Matron and Worthy Patron and anytime you are speaking in the Chapter room. Interlock your fingers and rest them on your abdomen.

ATTITUDE OF PRAYER AND REVERENT ATTITUDE

When the Bible is open on the Altar, it creates a holy area between it and the East and no one is permitted to walk between them except during the Initiation Ceremony or Installation of Officers.

The Labyrinth is the pentagon shaped area around the Star Points with the Altar in the center. The Reverent Attitude is assumed during Opening and Closing Ceremonies. While praying, clasp hands loosely, left hand palm up and the right palm laid over it held at waist level.

Ten Ways to Kill a Chapter

1. Don't come to meetings – But if you do, come late.
2. If the weather doesn't suit you, don't think of coming.
3. If you do not attend meetings, find fault with the work of the members and officers who do attend.
4. When asked to help, "Pass the Buck" to others.
5. Never accept an office (it is easier to criticize than do things).
6. Nevertheless, get sore if you are not appointed on a committee, but if you are, do not attend the meetings or do anything.
7. If asked by a chairperson to give your opinion on some important matter tell him you have nothing to say. After the meeting tell everybody how it should be run.
8. Do nothing more than is absolutely necessary, but when other members roll up their sleeves and willingly and unselfishly use their ability to help matters along, howl that the organization is run by a clique.
9. Don't bother to get new member, "Let the other fellows do that."
10. Never pay any dues. Show up once in a while – you might get something for nothing.

GAVEL USAGE

WHAT DO THE 1, 2, AND 3 GAVEL RAPS MEAN?

(Ritual page 51)

On Blow of the Gavel: *

Calls the Chapter to Order

Seats the Chapter when standing

Establishes a decision

Completes the closing of the Chapter

Two blows of the Gavel. **

Calls up the Officers

Three blows of the Gavel ***

Calls up everyone in the room

General Questions of the Order

GENERAL QUESTIONS

QUESTION	ANSWER
1. What is the purpose of an Eastern Star Chapter?	1. It is a school for the practice of self-control, good manners and all of the virtues of graces.
2. What was the name of the first secret society imitating Masonry?	2. "The Order of Perfect Happiness", organized in France in 1730.
3. What is the theory of the O.E.S. is founded upon?	3. The Holy Bible
4. What is the Order dedicated to?	4. Charity, Truth, and Loving Kindness
5. What is the year of establishment of the O.E.S.?	5. 1778
6. What two men are associated with the establishment of the O.E.S.?	6. Robert Morris and Robert Macoy
7. What is the inspiration of the O.E.S.?	7. The Star of Bethlehem
8. What is the mission of the Order?	8. Service
9. What is our work on earth?	9. To prepare the world to see His Star in the East.
10. The Star is a symbol for what?	10. Light or great intellectuality; a symbol for God
11. What is a symbol?	11. A figure used to represent a truth or fact.
12. How long have signs and symbols been used?	12. Since the time God set His rainbow in the sky.
13. What is a Landmark?	13. Certain fundamental or basic principles upon with the Order is founded
14. What Masonic Jurisdiction has outlawed the O.E.S:	14. The Grand Lodge of Pennsylvania
15. What is the least number of persons necessary to organize a chapter?	15. Seven
16. How many are necessary to confer degrees?	16. Nine
17. What key unlocks the doors of the Chapter as far as a petitioner is concerned?	17. The ballot
18. A chapter is like a garden of beautiful flowers. What instrument is it the duty of every Star to use to keep weeds out?	18. The ballot
19. What is a pentagon?	19. A figure having five strait sides
20. What does the pentagon represent?	20. The human body

21. What five stages of man does the pentagon outline?	21. Birth, Life, Death, Resurrection, and Ascension
22. What do the five lines outside the Star represent?	22. The Five Senses
23. What is the Signet?	23. A chart depicting the emblems of O.E.S.
24. The Five Points of the Star designate what?	24. The five statuses of woman; daughter, wife, widow, sister, and mother
25. What are the O.E.S. symbols made up of?	25. Straight lines, circle, and figures
26. What are the central points of the Star made up of?	26. Triangles
27. What is the equilateral triangle symbolic of?	27. God
28. What do the sides of an equilateral triangle signify?	28. All Knowing Wisdom, All Mighty Power, and All Embracing Love
29. What is the symbol for suffering?	29. The Cross
30. In what two degrees does the Lily appear as an emblem?	30. Ruth and Esther
31. What do the initial "A.O." stand for?	31. Anno Ordinis (In the year of the Order)
32. Why does the W.M. sit in the East?	32. The East has long been deemed the source of all light or wisdom
33. What is the badge of the W.M.?	33. The gavel
34. What is the Symbolism of the A.M. seat in the West?	34. Farewell, the close of life, the end of time, the afterglow of the meeting
35. What is the W.P.'s job in the Chapter?	35. To advise with other officers and to preside during the conferring of degrees
36. What is the W.M.'s gavel the symbol of?	36. Authority and Power
37. What essential characteristic should the W.M. have?	37. Self-control

Symbolism of 3-5-7

Here is a list of symbolisms of 3-5-7. Just to name a few. In all Eastern Star work we find that numbers are used to convey certain ideas or plans.

See if you can come up with additional symbolisms that are not listed.

THREE
- The Order of Eastern Star is dedicated to 3 things: Charity, Truth and Loving Kindness
- Each sign is given in 3 distinct motions
- The grip is given with 3 distinct movements
- There are 3 words in each of the passes
- Jesus was persecuted for 3 days
- Jesus laid in the tomb for 3 days
- There are 3 great events in a person's life - Birth, Life, Death

FIVE
- There are 5 raps at the door
- There are 5 points to the Star
- There are 5 emblematic colors
- There are 5 emblems and symbols
- There are 5 letters in the cabalistic word
- There are 5 signs and degrees
- There are 5 words in the cabalistic motto
- There are 5 degrees of relationship of women to a Master Mason

SEVEN
- There are 7 ties to the obligation
- 7 officers give instructions
- 7 members constitute a quorum
- Candidates are present to 7 stations
- 7 represent a number of completeness

Symbolic Ritual

The symbolic ritual of the Order of the Eastern Star is based on five famous religious heroines: Adah, Ruth,

Esther, Electa, and Martha. The degrees of the Order of the Eastern Star teach lessons of fidelity, constancy, loyalty, faith and love. These degrees are presented in a beautiful ritualistic ceremony designed to not only teach the lessons, but also to provide insight for future study and understanding. Unlike Blue Lodge Freemasonry, this ritual is based on actual historical events in the lives of these women, and the moral truth that was evidenced by them. The Order of the Eastern Star is centered around a Judea-Christian religious tradition.

Purpose: The stated purposes of the organization are: Charitable, Educational, Fraternal and Scientific; but there is much more to it than that. Dr. Rob Morris, the Poet Laureate of Masonry, founded the Order using beautiful and inspiring biblical examples of heroic conduct and moral values. These portray the noble principles which should adorn the personal lives of Eastern Star members. Eastern Star strives to take good people and through uplifting and elevating associations of love and service, and through precept and example, build an Order which is truly dedicated to charity, truth and loving kindness.

The Chair states, "*Sis. Jones wishes to withdraw the motion. Are there any objections?*" If none, the Chair declares the motion withdrawn. If there is any objection, a motion is presented (no second needed) and there is no discussion. The chair would immediately call for the question.

A motion placed before the meeting may be withdrawn by the mover provided it has not been stated by the Chair, because it does not belong to the assembly. If the motion has been moved, seconded, and stated by the Chair, it may be withdrawn by the mover (approval of seconder not needed), as long as there is no objection from the floor.

Amending a Motion

Sometimes questions call for the motion to be changed from its original form. The amendment takes precedence to the main motion to which it applies. Follow the same procedures to vote on amendment then incorporate amendment into main motion.

After the discussion is over as to how to amend the motion, it will have to be resubmitted to the body as follows: (example) "*Worthy Matron. I Sister, _____, move that we amend the motion to accept the minutes as read with the necessary corrections and the bills be forwarded to the Grand Chapter for payment*"

How to make amendments:

1. Adding: "*I move to amend the motion by adding the word(s) _____ at the end of the motion.*"
2. Striking (omitting): "*I move to amend the motion by striking the word(s)_____ sentence or paragraph.*"
3. Striking (substituting): "*I move to amend the motion by inserting the word(s) _____ after the word_____ and substituting the word(s), sentence or paragraph.*"
4. Inserting: "*I move to amend the motion by inserting the word(s), sentence or paragraph before or after the word _____.*"
5. Substituting: "*I move to amend the motion by substituting the following _____.*"

Always begin amendment with the words "*I move to amend the motion*" so the assembly is aware of your intent. You may move to amend the amendment, but only one such amendment can be on the floor at any one time. As true with any motions be prepared to speak for your amendment. The Chair has to read the motion as it stands after the amendment. It is important for the assembly to know what they are being asked to consider. The Chair should be sure that he/she has everyone's attention before the amended motion is read. In accepting any amendment, the chair must be careful that the purpose of the main motion is not lost.

BIBLE VERSES EVERY EASTERN STAR SHOULD KNOW

Genesis 1:3 (King James Version)

³And God said, Let there be light: and there was light.

Psalm 133 (King James Version)

¹Behold, how good and how pleasant it is for brethren to dwell together in unity!

² It is like the precious ointment upon the head, that ran down upon the beard, even Aaron's beard: that went down to the skirts of his garments;

³ As the dew of Hermon, and as the dew that descended upon the mountains of Zion: for there the LORD commanded the blessing, even life for evermore.

Matthew 2:2 (King James Version)

²Saying, Where is he that is born King of the Jews? for we have seen his star in the east, and are come to worship him.

Revelation 21:19 (King James Version)

¹⁹And the foundations of the wall of the city were garnished with all manner of precious stones. The first foundation was jasper; the second, sapphire; the third, a chalcedony; the fourth, an emerald;

Song of Solomon 5:9-16 (King James Version)

⁹What is thy beloved more than another beloved, O thou *fairest among* women? what is thy beloved more than another beloved, that thou dost so charge us?

¹⁰ My beloved is white and ruddy, the chiefest among ten *thousand*.

¹¹ His head is as the most fine gold, his locks are bushy, and black as a raven.

¹² His eyes are as the eyes of doves by the rivers of waters, washed with milk, and fitly set.

¹³ His cheeks are as a bed of spices, as sweet flowers: his lips like lilies, dropping sweet smelling myrrh.

¹⁴ His hands are as gold rings set with the beryl: his belly is as bright ivory overlaid with sapphires.

¹⁵ His legs are as pillars of marble, set upon sockets of fine gold: his countenance is as Lebanon, excellent as the cedars.

¹⁶ His mouth is most sweet: yea, he is *altogether lovely*. This is my beloved, and this is my friend, O daughters of Jerusalem.

OFFICES AND DUTIES

The duties of the Worthy Matron shall be to open and preside over the Chapter during its deliberations, to see the by-laws are promptly enforced, that the returns of the work of the Chapter are made annually to the Grand Chapter, and that the purposes of the Chapter are properly accomplished. She shall oversee all study sessions and is responsible for the Chapter's continuous learning of the Order. The Worthy Matron may, at times, appoint another member to preside or teach during a chapter study session. In the event of the dissolution of the Chapter, she shall promptly deliver all the Records, Books, Warrants, Rituals, etc. to the Grand Secretary for preservation.

The Worthy Patron (or a Master Mason recommended by the Worthy Patron) is to preside during the ceremony of initiation, and at the election and installation of officers, to assist the Worthy Matron in the performance of her duties, and to have supervisory care over the affairs of the Chapter.

The Associate Matron shall assist the Worthy Matron in the discharge of her duties and in the absence of the latter, shall preside and assume all the responsibilities of that office.

The Treasurer shall receive all monies, deposit the same in her name as Treasurer in a bank selected by the members, keep a just and regular account thereof, and pay out the same by order of the Worthy Matron and Secretary, with the consent of the Chapter. She shall report monthly to the Chapter the amount of her receipts and expenditures by item. At the expiration of her term, she shall deliver all money, books, papers, receipts, checking account information on, and other property belonging of the Chapter to her successor in office.

The Financial Secretary shall keep financial record of all dues, taxes and/or assessments for the Chapter. Collect monies at meetings and issues receipts, inform all members of the amount of their indebtedness and perform such other duties as may be required of her by the Worthy Matron of the Chapter. At the expiration of her term of office, she shall deliver books, papers, and other property belonging to the Chapter, to her successor in office.

The Recording Secretary shall record the proceedings of the Chapter and keep an accurate account between the Chapter and its members. She shall also issues notices and summons for meetings, read correspondence and renders a complete statement of the labor of the Chapter to the Grand Secretary of the Grand Chapter. She shall keep a register: of all the members of the Chapter, notify all committees of the appointment and perform such other duties as may be required of her by the Worthy Matron of the Chapter. At the expiration of her term of office, she shall deliver books, papers, and other property belonging to the Chapter, to her successor in office.

The Conductress shall receive and conduct all candidates through the ceremonies of the order. She is also responsible for setting up and breaking down the Chapter room in preparation of formal meetings.

The Associate Conductress shall be in charge of the preparation of candidates for ceremonies of the Order, assist the Conductress in her duties, and perform such duties as ascertained to her office and as may be required by the Matron and Conductress. She is also responsible for the set up and breakdown of the Chapter room after formal meetings.

Signs and Passes

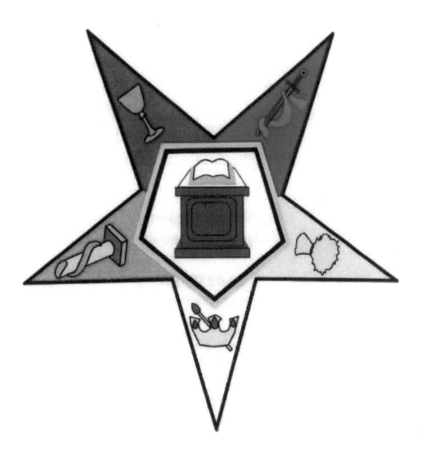

ADAH

1ˢᵗ POINT OF THE STAR

Degree	Daughter
Meaning	Ornament
Color	Blue
Flower	Violet
Emblem	Sword & Veil
Symbol	Open Bible

PASS
Alas, my daughter!
(Spoken by Jephthah)

BEATITUDE
Blessed are the pure in heart for they shall see GOD.

JEWEL
Turquoise

SEASON
Spring

2nd POINT OF THE STAR

Degree	Widow
Meaning	Friend
Color	Yellow
Flower	Jasmine
Emblem	Sheaf of Barley
Symbol	Lily of Valley

PASS

Who is this?

(Spoken by Boaz)

BEATITUDE

Blessed are the meek for they shall inherit the earth.

JEWEL

Topaz

SEASON

Summer

ESTHER

3rd POINT OF THE STAR

Degree	Wife
Meaning	Star
Color	White
Flower	White Lily
Emblem	Crown & Scepter
Symbol	Sun

PASS
What wilt thou?

BEATITUDE
Blessed are the peacemakers for they shall be called the children of GOD.

JEWEL
Diamond

SEASON

MARTHA

4th POINT OF THE STAR

Degree	Sister
Meaning	Instructed by Christ Abiding
Color	Green
Flower	Fern or Evergreen
Emblem	Broken Column
Symbol	Lamb & Cross

PASS
Believes thou this?

BEATITUDE
Blessed are them that mourn, for they shall be comforted.

JEWEL
Emerald

SEASON
Winter

ELECTA

5th POINT OF THE STAR

Degree	Mother
Meaning	Honorable called of God
Color	Red
Flower	Red Rose
Emblem	Cup
Symbol	Lion

PASS
Love one another?
(Spoken by John the Apostle)

BEATITUDE
Blessed are they which are persecuted for righteousness sake for theirs is the kingdom of heaven.

JEWEL
Ruby

SEASON
Autumn

Charts of the Order

ADAH

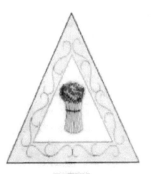

RUTH

RUTH

MARTHA

ELECTA

HOW TO PROTECT YOUR EMBLEM

QUESTION	ANSWER
Are you a member of the Order of the Eastern Star?	I have seen His Star in the East.
What do you do here?	I have come to worship Him.
What further evidence do you have to prove yourself as an Eastern Star?	I have six signs, five passes and two mottoes, one general, the other a Special motto, a word and a grip.
What is the general motto?	I have seen His star in the East and have come to worship Him.
What is the special motto?	Fairest among thousands altogether lovely.
What are the five heroines of the Order?	Adah, Ruth, Esther, Martha, and Electa
What are their colors?	Blue, Yellow, White, Green, and Red
What color is Adah?	Blue
What color is Ruth?	Yellow
What color is Esther?	White
What color is Martha?	Green
What color is Electa?	Red
What are the five flowers of the Order?	Violet, Yellow Jasmine, White Lily, Fern, and Red Rose
What do they teach?	Violet – Faithful, Yellow Jasmine – Constant White Lily – Pure Fern – Hopeful Red Rose – Frequent
What does the blue point represent?	Faithfulness
What does the yellow point represent?	Steadfastness
What does the white point represent?	Pure, Hope and Light
What does the green point represent?	Hope in Immortality
What does the red point represent?	Frequent and Zeal

Can you name the central division of the star?	The open bible is appropriate to Jephthah's daughter as obedience to God. The bunch of lilies is appropriate to Ruth as lily of the valley. The Refulgent sun is appropriate to Esther as a symbol of crown and majesty. The lamb and cross is appropriate to Martha as a symbol of innocence, faith and humility. The lion is appropriate to Electa as a symbol of courage and strength which sustained her during her severe trials.
Can you name the emblems of each point of the star?	Adah – Sword and Veil Ruth – Sheaves of barley Esther – Crown and scepter Martha – Broken Column Electa – The cup of bitter draught
How many knocks does it take the enter the chapter after it is opened?	5
What do they represent?	The Five Heroines of the Order
How many officers does it take to constitute a Chapter of the Eastern Star?	14
Name them?	Worthy Matron, Worthy Patron, Associate Matron, Treasurer, Secretary, Conductress, Associate Conductress, Warder Sentinel, Adah, Ruth, Esther, Martha and Electa
Will you give me the password of the Order?	I will with your assistance...
Begin?	Nay, you begin.
F.	A.
T.	A.
Both: L	The word is _____

Order of Eastern Star

Study Guide

Here is a general breakdown of each star point. You should be familiar with this information as well as be able to recite it at my time.

Pentagon	Cabalistic Word	Ideals/ Virtue	Heroine	Degree	Meaning	Color	Season	Flower	Jewel	Emblem	Christ Symbols	Pass	Beatitude
Birth	F	Faithful	Adah/ Jephthah's Daughter	Daughter	Ornament	Blue	Spring	Violet	Turquoise	Sword & Veil	Open Bible	Alas, my Daughter Judges 11:35	Blessed are the pure in heart for they shall see God.
Life	A	Constancy	Ruth	Widow	Friend	Yellow	Summer	Jasmine	Topaz	Sheaf of Barley	Lily of Valley	Who is This? Ruth 2:5	Blessed are the meek for they shall inherit the earth.
Death	T	Pure	Ester	Wife	Star	White	---	White Lily	Diamond	Crown & Scepter	Sun	What Wilt thou? Esther 5:3	Blessed are the peace makers for they shall be called the Children of God.
Resurrection	A	Hopeful	Martha	Sister	Instructed by Christ	Green	Winter	Fern	Emerald	Broken Column	Lamb & Cross	Believest Thou This! John 11:26	Blessed are them that mourn for they shall be comforted.
Ascension	L	Fervent	Electa/ Elect Lady	Mother	Honorable Called of God	Red	Autumn	Red Rose	Ruby	Cup	Lion	Love One Another 2 John 1:5	Blessed are they which are persecute for righteousness sake for theirs is the kingdom of heaven.

30

Jewel and Emblem of Each Officer

TITLE	EMBLEM	JEWEL
Worthy Matron	Gavel	Jasper
Worthy Patron	Square and Compass	Sapphire
Associate Matron	Refulgent Sun	Chalcedony
Associate Patron	Rayed Star	
Secretary	Crossed Pens	Emerald
Treasurer	Crossed Keys	Sardonyx
Conductress	Scroll and Baton	Sardius
Associate Conductress	Baton	Chrysolyte
Chaplain	Open Bible	Beryl
Marshal	Crossed Batons	Olivene
Musician	Lyre	Chrysoprasus; Chrysoberyl
Trustee	Key	
Adah	Sword and Veil	Turquoise
Ruth	Sheaf of Barley	Yellow Topaz
Esther	Crown and Sceptre	Diamond
Martha	Broken Column	Emerald
Electa	Cup	Ruby
Warder	Dove	
Sentinel	Crossed Swords	
Christian Flag Bearer	Christian Flag	
US Flag Bearer	US Flag	
OES Flag Bearer	OES Flag	

Revelation 21:19 KJV

31

BIBLICAL RELATIONSHIP TO THE EASTERN STARS

The Beatitudes

Heroine	Beatitude	Scripture
ADAH	6th	"Blessed are the pure in heart, for they shall see GOD"
RUTH	3rd	"Blessed are the meek for they shall inherit the earth"
ESTHER	7th	"Blessed are the peacemaker, for they shall be called the children of GOD"
MARTHA	2nd	"Blessed are they that mourn for they shall be comforted"
ELECTA	8th	"Blessed are ye, when men shall revile you, and persecute you and hall all manner of evil against you falsely for my sake"

*10 Total found in Matthew Chapter 5

The Four Seasons

Heroine	Season	Symbolizes
ADAH	Spring	Symbolizing youth of life
RUTH	Summer	Symbolizing abundance and growth of life
ELECTA	Autumn	Symbolizing harvest or the period of full maturity of life
MARTHA	Winter	Symbolizing the end of the year, or lifetime when one must rely on eternal life

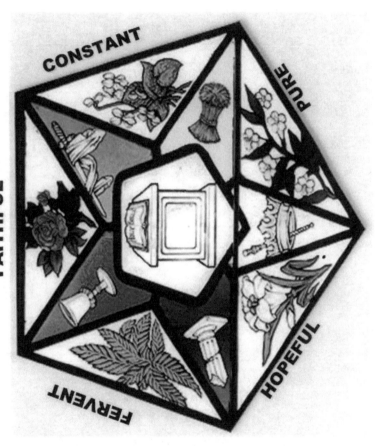

CONSTANT

PURE

FAITHFUL

FERVENT

HOPEFUL

THE FIVE HEROINES OF THE ORDER OF EASTERN STAR

NAME	ADAH	RUTH	ESTHER	MARTHA	ELECTA
DEGREE	Daughter	Widow	Wife	Sister	Mother
PLACE	Gilead	Bethlehem	Persia	Bethany	Rome
FOUND IN BIBLE	Judges 11	Ruth	Esther	St. John	St. John
COLOR	Blue	Yellow	White	Green	Red
EMBLEM	Sword & Veil	Sheaf of Wheat	Crown & Sceptre	Broken Column	Cup
PASS	Alas my daughter	Who is this?	What wilt thou?	Believest thou this?	Love one another
FLOWER	Blue Violet	Yellow Jasmine	White Lily	Fern	Red Rose
JEWEL	Turquoise	Yellow Topaz	Diamond	Emerald	Ruby
SYMBOL	Open Bible	Lily of the Valley	Sun	Lamb & Cross	Lion
SEASON	Spring	Summer		Winter	Autumn
IDEALS	Self-Sacrifice, Integrity and Obedience	Loyalty and Friendship	Purity and Self-Sacrifice	Faith, Belief in Eternal Life and Belief in Immorality of the Soul	Love and Hospitality
MEANING OF NAME	Ornament	Friend	Star	Abiding Faith; Fortitude; Instructed by Christ	Called of God; Overseer
RELATION	Jephthah	Mahlon	King Xerses (Ahasuerus)	Lazarus	Adrian/David
YEAR	BC 1148	BC 1332	BC 51	AD 33	AD 90
VIRTUE	Loyalty	Constancy	Purity	Hope	Fervency
S-E-R-V-E	Steadfast	Endurance	Royalty	Victory	Electoralship
LESSONS TAUGHT	To be steadfast in our vows	The value of true friendship and loyalty	Willingness to sacrifice and faithfulness to kindred and friends	Faith and belief in eternal life	Patience and submission under wrongs of persecution
BEATITUTED	Blessed are the pure in heart for they shall see God. (Matthew 5:8)	Blessed are the meek for they shall inherit the earth. (Matthew 5:5)	Blessed are the peacemakers: for they shall be called the children of God. (Matthew 5:9)	Blessed are them that mourn. For they shall be comforted. (Matthew 5:4)	Blessed are they which are persecuted for righteousness' sake: for theirs is the kingdom of heaven. (Matthew 5:10)

34

Chapter
set up

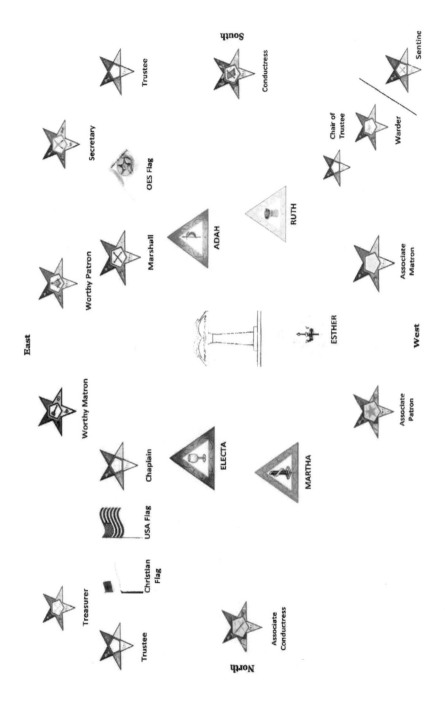

East

West

North

South

Trustee

Secretary

OES Flag

Worthy Patron

Marshall

ADAH

RUTH

Chair of Trustee

Warder

Sentine

Associate Matron

ESTHER

Conductress

Worthy Matron

Chaplain

ELECTA

MARTHA

Associate Patron

USA Flag

Treasurer

Christian Flag

Trustee

Associate Conductress

37

Chapter Room Set-Up

Always tell the truth even If it makes everyone cry

(ATTTEMEC)

Associate Conductress

Treasurer

Trustee

Electa

Martha

Esther

Chair of Trustee

Cousin Stacy made me tell Adah right from wrong

(CSMTARW)

Conductress

Secretary

Marshall

Trustee

Adah

Ruth

Warder

ALTAR

(Chaplain)

WM   AM

38

Emblems

WORTHY MATRON - Gravel within the Star
Symbolizes the power and authority of the East.

ASSOCIATE MATRON - Refulgent Sun within the Star
Symbolizes that this officer should be a source of enlightenment and that she should have a personality which literally radiates from the light received from the East.

WORTHY PATRON - Square and Compass within the Star
Symbolizes the fax that there is a necessity to double our efforts to bring the light of the Star into our lives.

SECRETARY - Crossed Pens within the Star
Symbolically the two pens represents the fact that our deeds may be either good or band and that our deeds are recorded on a higher record, thus, the one pen is a pen of COMMENDATION, the other pen of CONDEMNATION.

TREASURER - Crossed Keys within the Star
Represents the safety and security of the resources of the Chapter.

CONDUCTRESS - Scroll & Baton within the Star
Represent plans carefully made and well executed.

ASSOCIATE CONDUCTRESS - Baton within the Star
Represents discipline.

CHAPLAIN - Open Bible within the Star
Represents the need for the word of God in the work of the chapter and in the life of the individual. The Open Bible is also the symbol of Adah.

TRUSTEE - Key within the Star

MARSHALL - Crossed Baton within the Star
Symbolizes service as the highest expression of love.

ADAH – Sword & Veil

Symbolizes the Right and the Revelation, it represents the concept that the Sword must sometimes be taken up in the defense of right and in the performance of duty. The Word of Christ was described as a two edged sword. The Sword is what Jephthah held, and the veil is what Adah wore.

RUTH – Golden Sheaf

Emphasizes the worth of small tasks and humble duties in the eyes of God. The small acts of kindness and the patience of laboring which characterized Ruth's life were as suitable gifts to God as the sheaves which she gleaned.

Emblem Recognition	
Worthy Matron	
Worthy Patron	
Associate Matron	
Associate Patron	
Secretary	
Treasurer	
Conductress	
Associate Conductress	

Chaplain	
Trustee	
Marshall	
Sentinel	
Warder	
Musician	
Past Matron	
Past Patron	

How to walk the labyrinth

HOW TO WALK THE LABYRINTH

Walk around the alter, to the right
And step out on **Adah**.
Walk thru **Electa**, around
Martha, thru **Esther** and to Ruth
Walk thru **Adah**, around **Electa**,
Thru Martha and to **Esther**.
Walk thru **Electa** and to **Martha**.
Walk thru **Esther**, around Ruth
Thru **Adah** and to **Electa**.
Walk thru **Martha**, around **Esther**
And step out of labyrinth in front of altar.

Stories of the
5
heroines

The 5 Points

Adah	*Sword and Veil within the Triangle*
Ruth	*Sheaf of wheat within the Triangle*
Esther	*Crown and Scepter within the Triangle*
Martha	*Broken Column within the Triangle*
Esther	**The Cup within the Triangle**

Adah

First point of the star. My duty is to make known to all proper inquiries the light knowledge and beauty of the blue ray, which represents the clearness of the sky, when all clouds have vanished, and symbolizes chastity, loyalty, fidelity and a spotless reputation. My emblems are the Sword and veil, emblematic of the heroic conduct of Jephthah's Daughter, whom I represent.

Ruth

Second point of the star. My duty is to make known to all proper inquiries the light knowledge and beauty of the yellow ray, which symbolizes constancy, purity and the lustre of great brightness. My badge, the Sheaf, is an emblem of plenty, which being composed of distinct and great parts, is gathered together by patient industry. Such was the generous labor of the humble gleaner, Ruth, whom I represent.

Esther

Third point of the star. My duty is to make known to all proper inquiries the light knowledge and beauty of the white ray, which symbolizes light, purity and joy. My badge, the Crown and Scepter united, is an emblem of royalty and power. In the exercise of high authority, we should be governed by the purest principles of justices and moderation. It was by the practice of these attributes that Esther, whom I represent, saved her people from extirpation.

Martha

Fourth point in the star. My duty is to make known to all proper inquiries the light knowledge and beauty of the green ray, the purity and freshness of which are emblems of delight – the beauties of nature – symbolizing hope immorality. My badge, the Broken Column, is typical of the death of a human being, but down in the vigor of manhood and express the sisterly grief of Martha, whom I represent.

Electa

Fifth point of the star. My duty is to make known to all proper inquiries the light knowledge and beauty of the red ray, symbolically representing ardor and zeal, which should actuate all who are engaged in the Holy cause of benevolence. My badge, the Cup, is an emblem of the bitter draught of which we are constantly partaking through lift, but however distasteful, will in the end, overflow with blessing rich, abounding and eternal.

Story of
Adah

Adah

Definition	Ornament
Degree	Daughter
Gem	Turquoise
Flower	Violet
Teaching	Faithful
Emblem	Sword & Veil
Color	Blue (Faithfulness)
Beatitude	6th Beatitude (Matthew 5:8)
Verse Reference	Judges 11
Song	Walk With Me
Season	Spring
Pass	Alas, My Daughter

ADAH

1ˢᵗ POINT OF THE STAR

Degree	Daughter
Meaning	Ornament
Color	Blue
Flower	Violet
Emblem	Sword & Veil
Symbol	Open Bible

PASS
Alas, my daughter!
(Spoken by Jephthah)

BEATITUDE
Blessed are the pure in heart for they shall see GOD.

JEWEL
Turquoise

SEASON
Spring

ADAH

The Lesson of the Daughter

Let me state in the beginning that the name of Adah does not appear in the Bible, that she is always referred to as Jephthah's daughter and that "Adah" was the name given her by the founder of our Order, Dr. Robert Morris.

The story of Adah is based upon the tragedy of a race that forgot God. It was in the 12th Century, B.C. that Israel had strayed away from God, had practiced idolatry and in every way showed their contempt for His laws; and for their sins God had delivered them into the hands of their enemies, the Ammonites and the Philistines, who laid waste to their country.

In the midst of this calamity Jephthah, a born organizer and leader, who had been made an outcast in his own country in a family feud, gathered a formidable army of men of a similar social standing (beggars, thieves and outlaws) and by a rigid training brought them under the strictest discipline, and thus became an expert in the tactics of warfare.

After suffering severe calamities, Israel put away their idols and strange gods, and humbled themselves before the God of heaven and besought Him with prayers and sacrifices to deliver them from the hand of the enemy. And the Lord, whose ear is ever open to the cry of His children, heard them and sent them a deliverer. They had an army, untrained and without a leader, and it was at this crisis that the elders of Israel, some of them even were Jephthah's brothers, went to Jephthah and implored him to be their leader. This was a bitter pill for these brothers to approach an outcast member of their family, but in a case of absolute necessity family feuds must be forgotten and even principles must be reevaluated.

Jephthah himself was greatly surprised, and it required considerable persuasion to secure his assistance, because his prejudices had been deeply grounded, and "the stone which the builders had rejected was become the headstone of the corner," even against the old Jewish law which would have forbidden him to rule the nation because of his lowly birth. And so a solemn compact was entered into whereby if Jephthah should be victorious over their enemies, he was to become the recognized leader of the nation.

Now Jephthah realized that of his own power and strength he could not accomplish the task that lay before him, and so he besought the Lord to help him with prayers and sacrifices. And then a mighty thing happened; the Spirit of the Lord came upon Jephthah, and he no longer attempted to make peace with his enemies by sending messengers back and forth, but he marshaled his forces and passed in triumphant tread to face them in open battle.

And then came this memorable vow. We are impressed with his statement to the Ammonites when he said: "Jehovah, the Judge, be judge this day between children of Israel and the children of Ammon." It was at the altar in Mizpah, it would seem, that he -went and made a solemn vow to the Lord and said: "If thou wilt indeed deliver the children of Ammon into my hand, then it shall be, that whosoever cometh forth from the doors of my house to meet me, when I return in peace from the children of Ammon, it shall be Jehovah's, and I will offer it up for a burnt offering."

Now why was this vow made? Did his faith falter at the last moment - did it seem incredible that God should use him in his deliverance of the Israelites from their enemy? Or was it a mere expression of a grateful heart for blessings received?

The battled followed. The enemy was pursued into the very heart of their country. Twenty cities were conquered, and the whole country completely subdued. But at what price! Jephthah was soon to realize the truth of what the victory would cost him. That vow!

We can well picture him as he returns in triumph to Mizpah. No doubt in a brazen chariot, accompanied by armor-clad warriors, and the streets filled with a joyous and jubilant people.

But how soon a joyous victory was to be returned into grief and distress. True at heart in adversity, he was also true in prosperity, and the vow he had made when he besought the strong arm of the Lord was lost to him when he beheld his beloved daughter, the very core of his heart, his idolized child, rush out to greet him in his triumphant entry, and the vow he had uttered flashed across his mind. Jephthah presents a noble example of fidelity to his word, for he never for one moment entertained the thought of trying to avoid the fulfillment of his vow. We are deeply impressed by the overwhelming grief of Jephthah and the noble self-sacrifice of his daughter Adah, and her courageous resignation to her fate. Jephthah's daughter arose at once to the grandeur of her situation and bade her father keep his promise. She made one humble request: "Let me alone for two months, and I may depart and go down :o the mountains, I and my companions."

Jephthah's Daughter	To Adah "Obedience"
Father, father, the joyful minstrel sung – Lo, glad I come with timbrel and with dance; Hail, father, hail! Thine arm in God was strong. Hail, God of Israel, Israel's sure defense. Hosanna! Hosanna! Thus the minstrel sung. Father, father! The astonished daughter cried – What grief is this? What means this sign of wo? Dust on thy head! Thy grey hairs floating wide! That look of horror on each soldier's bow -- Bewailing, bewailing – Thus the daughter cried. Father, father! The maid devoted said – If thus I'm doomed, if thus thy vow has gone, Oh turn not back! There's hope amidst the dead, None for the perjured – let thy will be done, Hosanna! Hosanna! Thus the maiden said. Father, father! The doomed one meekly spoke – Be strong thy hand, be resolute thy heart – To heaven's re-union I will joyful look, And with a blessing on thy head depart. Farewell! Farewell! Thus the Doomed One spoke. -Rob Morris	Our Star life's not always easy, We do need rare courage now, Like that young, heroic Adah, Keeping her father's awful vow. We obey, as she has taught us, Sometime cry o'er life's ills; But steadfast we turn our faces Far from Adah's lonely hills. This world has obedient daughter, Carrying out a hard command; We must seek them – weary, troubled, Life them with a true "Star" hand. Their quiet trust and true obedience Are examples naught can mar. Bring a candle of rare courage To the first point of our Star.

Judges 11 New International Version (NIV)

11 Jephthah the Gileadite was a mighty warrior. His father was Gilead; his mother was a prostitute. ²Gilead's wife also bore him sons, and when they were grown up, they drove Jephthah away. "You are not going to get any inheritance in our family," they said, "because you are the son of another woman." ³So Jephthah fled from his brothers and settled in the land of Tob, where a gang of scoundrels gathered around him and followed him.

⁴Some time later, when the Ammonites were fighting against Israel, ⁵the elders of Gilead went to get Jephthah from the land of Tob. ⁶"Come," they said, "be our commander, so we can fight the Ammonites."

⁷Jephthah said to them, "Didn't you hate me and drive me from my father's house? Why do you come to me now, when you're in trouble?"

⁸The elders of Gilead said to him, "Nevertheless, we are turning to you now; come with us to fight the Ammonites, and you will be head over all of us who live in Gilead."

⁹Jephthah answered, "Suppose you take me back to fight the Ammonites and the LORD gives them to me—will I really be your head?"

¹⁰The elders of Gilead replied, "The LORD is our witness; we will certainly do as you say." ¹¹So Jephthah went with the elders of Gilead, and the people made him head and commander over them. And he repeated all his words before the LORD in Mizpah.

¹²Then Jephthah sent messengers to the Ammonite king with the question: "What do you have against me that you have attacked my country?"

¹³The king of the Ammonites answered Jephthah's messengers, "When Israel came up out of Egypt, they took away my land from the Arnon to the Jabbok, all the way to the Jordan. Now give it back peaceably."

¹⁴Jephthah sent back messengers to the Ammonite king, ¹⁵saying:

"This is what Jephthah says: Israel did not take the land of Moab or the land of the Ammonites. ¹⁶But when they came up out of Egypt, Israel went through the wilderness to the Red Sea⁽ᵃ⁾ and on to Kadesh. ¹⁷Then Israel sent messengers to the king of Edom, saying, 'Give us permission to go through your country,' but the king of Edom would not listen. They sent also to the king of Moab, and he refused. So Israel stayed at Kadesh.

¹⁸"Next they traveled through the wilderness, skirted the lands of Edom and Moab, passed along the eastern side of the country of Moab, and camped on the other side of the Arnon. They did not enter the territory of Moab, for the Arnon was its border.

¹⁹"Then Israel sent messengers to Sihon king of the Amorites, who ruled in Heshbon, and said to him, 'Let us pass through your country to our own place.' ²⁰Sihon, however, did not trust Israel[c] to pass through his territory. He mustered all his troops and encamped at Jahaz and fought with Israel.

²¹"Then the LORD, the God of Israel, gave Sihon and his whole army into Israel's hands, and they defeated them. Israel took over all the land of the Amorites who lived in that country, ²²capturing all of it from the Arnon to the Jabbok and from the desert to the Jordan.

²³"Now since the LORD, the God of Israel, has driven the Amorites out before his people Israel, what right have you to take it over? ²⁴Will you not take what your god Chemosh gives you? Likewise, whatever the LORD our God has given us, we will possess. ²⁵Are you any better than Balak son of Zippor, king of Moab? Did he ever quarrel with Israel or fight with them? ²⁶For three hundred years Israel occupied Heshbon, Aroer, the surrounding settlements and all the towns along the Arnon. Why didn't you retake them during that time? ²⁷I have not wronged you, but you are doing me wrong by waging war against me. Let the LORD, the Judge, decide the dispute this day between the Israelites and the Ammonites."

²⁸The king of Ammon, however, paid no attention to the message Jephthah sent him.

²⁹Then the Spirit of the LORD came on Jephthah. He crossed Gilead and Manasseh, passed through Mizpah of Gilead, and from there he advanced against the Ammonites. ³⁰And Jephthah made a vow to the LORD: "If you give the Ammonites into my hands, ³¹whatever comes out of the door of my house to meet me when I return in triumph from the Ammonites will be the LORD's, and I will sacrifice it as a burnt offering."

³²Then Jephthah went over to fight the Ammonites, and the LORD gave them into his hands. ³³He devastated twenty towns from Aroer to the vicinity of Minnith, as far as Abel Keramim. Thus Israel subdued Ammon.

³⁴When Jephthah returned to his home in Mizpah, who should come out to meet him but his daughter, dancing to the sound of timbrels! She was an only child. Except for her he had neither son nor daughter. ³⁵When he saw her, he tore his clothes and cried, "Oh no,

my daughter! You have brought me down and I am devastated. I have made a vow to the LORD that I cannot break."

³⁶"My father," she replied, "you have given your word to the LORD. Do to me just as you promised, now that the LORD has avenged you of your enemies, the Ammonites. ³⁷But grant me this one request," she said. "Give me two months to roam the hills and weep with my friends, because I will never marry."

³⁸"You may go," he said. And he let her go for two months. She and her friends went into the hills and wept because she would never marry. ³⁹After the two months, she returned to her father, and he did to her as he had vowed. And she was a virgin.

From this comes the Israelite tradition ⁴⁰that each year the young women of Israel go out for four days to commemorate the daughter of Jephthah the Gileadite.

Judges 11 King James Version (KJV)

11 Now Jephthah the Gileadite was a mighty man of valour, and he was the son of an harlot: and Gilead begat Jephthah.

²And Gilead's wife bare him sons; and his wife's sons grew up, and they thrust out Jephthah, and said unto him, Thou shalt not inherit in our father's house; for thou art the son of a strange woman.

³Then Jephthah fled from his brethren, and dwelt in the land of Tob: and there were gathered vain men to Jephthah, and went out with him.

⁴And it came to pass in process of time, that the children of Ammon made war against Israel.

⁵And it was so, that when the children of Ammon made war against Israel, the elders of Gilead went to fetch Jephthah out of the land of Tob:

⁶And they said unto Jephthah, Come, and be our captain, that we may fight with the children of Ammon.

⁷And Jephthah said unto the elders of Gilead, Did not ye hate me, and expel me out of my father's house? and why are ye come unto me now when ye are in distress?

⁸And the elders of Gilead said unto Jephthah, Therefore we turn again to thee now, that thou mayest go with us, and fight against the children of Ammon, and be our head over all the inhabitants of Gilead.

⁹And Jephthah said unto the elders of Gilead, If ye bring me home again to fight against the children of Ammon, and the LORD deliver them before me, shall I be your head?

¹⁰And the elders of Gilead said unto Jephthah, The LORD be witness between us, if we do not so according to thy words.

¹¹Then Jephthah went with the elders of Gilead, and the people made him head and captain over them: and Jephthah uttered all his words before the LORD in Mizpeh.

¹²And Jephthah sent messengers unto the king of the children of Ammon, saying, What hast thou to do with me, that thou art come against me to fight in my land?

¹³And the king of the children of Ammon answered unto the messengers of Jephthah, Because Israel took away my land, when they came up out of Egypt, from Arnon even unto Jabbok, and unto Jordan: now therefore restore those lands again peaceably.

[14]And Jephthah sent messengers again unto the king of the children of Ammon:

[15]And said unto him, Thus saith Jephthah, Israel took not away the land of Moab, nor the land of the children of Ammon:

[16]But when Israel came up from Egypt, and walked through the wilderness unto the Red sea, and came to Kadesh;

[17]Then Israel sent messengers unto the king of Edom, saying, Let me, I pray thee, pass through thy land: but the king of Edom would not hearken thereto. And in like manner they sent unto the king of Moab: but he would not consent: and Israel abode in Kadesh.

[18]Then they went along through the wilderness, and compassed the land of Edom, and the land of Moab, and came by the east side of the land of Moab, and pitched on the other side of Arnon, but came not within the border of Moab: for Arnon was the border of Moab.

[19]And Israel sent messengers unto Sihon king of the Amorites, the king of Heshbon; and Israel said unto him, Let us pass, we pray thee, through thy land into my place.

[20]But Sihon trusted not Israel to pass through his coast: but Sihon gathered all his people together, and pitched in Jahaz, and fought against Israel.

[21]And the LORD God of Israel delivered Sihon and all his people into the hand of Israel, and they smote them: so Israel possessed all the land of the Amorites, the inhabitants of that country.

[22]And they possessed all the coasts of the Amorites, from Arnon even unto Jabbok, and from the wilderness even unto Jordan.

[23]So now the LORD God of Israel hath dispossessed the Amorites from before his people Israel, and shouldest thou possess it?

[24]Wilt not thou possess that which Chemosh thy god giveth thee to possess? So whomsoever the LORD our God shall drive out from before us, them will we possess.

[25]And now art thou any thing better than Balak the son of Zippor, king of Moab? did he ever strive against Israel, or did he ever fight against them,

[26]While Israel dwelt in Heshbon and her towns, and in Aroer and her towns, and in all the cities that be along by the coasts of Arnon, three hundred years? why therefore did ye not recover them within that time?

27 Wherefore I have not sinned against thee, but thou doest me wrong to war against me: the LORD the Judge be judge this day between the children of Israel and the children of Ammon.

28 Howbeit the king of the children of Ammon hearkened not unto the words of Jephthah which he sent him.

29 Then the Spirit of the LORD came upon Jephthah, and he passed over Gilead, and Manasseh, and passed over Mizpeh of Gilead, and from Mizpeh of Gilead he passed over unto the children of Ammon.

30 And Jephthah vowed a vow unto the LORD, and said, If thou shalt without fail deliver the children of Ammon into mine hands,

31 Then it shall be, that whatsoever cometh forth of the doors of my house to meet me, when I return in peace from the children of Ammon, shall surely be the LORD's, and I will offer it up for a burnt offering.

32 So Jephthah passed over unto the children of Ammon to fight against them; and the LORD delivered them into his hands.

33 And he smote them from Aroer, even till thou come to Minnith, even twenty cities, and unto the plain of the vineyards, with a very great slaughter. Thus the children of Ammon were subdued before the children of Israel.

34 And Jephthah came to Mizpeh unto his house, and, behold, his daughter came out to meet him with timbrels and with dances: and she was his only child; beside her he had neither son nor daughter.

35 And it came to pass, when he saw her, that he rent his clothes, and said, Alas, my daughter! thou hast brought me very low, and thou art one of them that trouble me: for I have opened my mouth unto the LORD, and I cannot go back.

36 And she said unto him, My father, if thou hast opened thy mouth unto the LORD, do to me according to that which hath proceeded out of thy mouth; forasmuch as the LORD hath taken vengeance for thee of thine enemies, even of the children of Ammon.

37 And she said unto her father, Let this thing be done for me: let me alone two months, that I may go up and down upon the mountains, and bewail my virginity, I and my fellows.

[38]And he said, Go. And he sent her away for two months: and she went with her companions, and bewailed her virginity upon the mountains.

[39]And it came to pass at the end of two months, that she returned unto her father, who did with her according to his vow which he had vowed: and she knew no man. And it was a custom in Israel,

[40]That the daughters of Israel went yearly to lament the daughter of Jephthah the Gileadite four days in a year.

ADAH - Ornament

QUESTION	ANSWER
Who was Jephthah?	The father of Adah and one of the Judges of Israel.
What was a Judge of Israel?	The men who served as leaders of Israel after Moses' and Joshua's time.
Who was Othneil?	Othneil was the first judge of Israel.
What nation did Jephthah make war against?	The Ammonites
Where was Jephthah when called to lead his people's army?	The Land of Tob.
At what place was Jephthah's home located?	Mizpeh
Where is the story of Adah found in the Bible?	Judges 11:29-40
What does the name Adah mean?	Ornament
Why has Jephthah's Daughter been named ADAH?	Because she was an ornament to her father.
Was Adah the only child?	Yes, The Bible says: "Besides her, he had neither son or daughter"
What other two Biblical women are named Adah?	The wife of Lamech, and the Daughter of Elon.
How many judges did Israel have?	Thirteen
What Judge was Jephthah?	Ninth
What was Jephthah's father named?	Gilead
Did Adah go to the mountains alone?	No, her companions went with her.
What did Adah do while in the mountains?	She bewailed her virginity.
Why did Adah lament her virginity?	It as the hope and secret desire of every Jewish maiden that she might become the mother of the Messiah.
Why did Adah lift her veil?	To show her innocence.
What instrument was used in the sacrifice of Adah?	The sword.
What yearly customs did Adah's sacrifice bring about?	For a period of four days each year, the daughters of Israel lamented for Adah.
What is the Point Emblem of this Degree?	The Sword & Veil
What is the Sword typical of?	The right dividing laws of God and the principals of man.
What is the Veil symbolic of?	Revelation
What does the lifting of the veil signify?	The gaining of spiritual light.
What is the Christ symbol in this degree?	The Bible, as the WORD.
What is the color of this degree symbolic of?	The sky and sea. Blue is symbolic of truth and faithfulness.

Adah

Adah is the first Star Point Heroine

REPRESENTS

It represents the Ideal Daughter because her sense of duty and devotion to her father so guided her actions that, by her deeds, exemplified the highest type of obedience.

THE MEANING OF THE NAME

The name "ADAH" means "ORNAMENT". Although the name Adah does not appear in the biblical story of Jephthah's daughter, it is an appropriate choice. Her innocent spirit and faultless character were her own personal ornaments, but it may also be said that a daughter who so exemplified those virtues was an ornament to her father's life.

COLOR

The clear blue skies is the color dedicated to the First Star Point. ___ ever the symbol of fidelity, loyalty and intelligence, represents __ her excellent use of her intellect in determine the right course of action and the unparalleled loyalty to her father.

FLOWER

The violet is dedicated to her because it is associated with meekness ____ humility. The violet represents the willing subjugation of personal desire and wishes in order that one's duty may be properly filled.

IDEALS

The ideals of the First Star Point are self-sacrifice, integrity, and obedience. These ideal characteristics may be achieved by emulating spirit and actions typified by the life of Adah.

EMBLEMS

The emblem of Adah is the Sword and Veil which represent Right and the Revelation. Right courses of action may be followed when the word of God is revealed or made known to the individual and accepted.

SYMBOL

The Open Bible is symbolic of the deeper meaning which is to be grasped. Therefore, only the Word of God may direct and individual in the right way to go.

61

JEWEL

The Turquoise, or the blue Sapphire, is used to represent the character traits exemplified by Adah. The turquoise indicates that if we wish to make our lives a shining Star, we must forever master the virtue of the Star Point, which is obedient loyalty.

SEASON

Adah represent the Spring of the year, because her life is representative of early womanhood of life itself. Her story challenges us to carry throughout our lives, the innocent and sweetness of a young girl and to approach life problems with enthusiasm and willingness.

BEATITUDE

The sixth beatitude is associated with Adah, "Blessed are the pure in heart: for they shall see God." Matthew 5:8

THE STORY

Judges 11:1-40

Every Conscientious Eastern Star, who continually probes and studies the lessons of our Order in search of meanings, is often perplexed by some staggering problems. Since Jephthah's vow involved the sacrifices of Adah, the offering that he made was subject to Leviticus Laws. There were definite laws which governed the redemption of human life which had been vowed as a sacrifice. The sacrifice of children was strictly forbidden.

Read --- Leviticus 27:1-4

Complied by Alberta W. Jones, G.M.

Story of
Ruth

Definition	Friend
Degree	Widow
Gem	Topaz
Flower	Yellow Jasmine
Teaching	Constant
Emblem	Sheaf of Wheat
Color	Yellow
	(Steadfast)
Beatitude	3rd Beatitude (Matthew 5:5)
Verse Reference	Book of Ruth
Song	Where He Lead Me
Season	Summer
Pass	Who is this?

RUTH

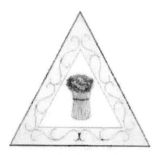

2nd *POINT OF THE STAR*

Degree	Widow
Meaning	Friend
Color	Yellow
Flower	Jasmine
Emblem	Sheaf of Barley
Symbol	Lily of Valley

PASS
Who is this?
(Spoken by Boaz)

BEATITUDE
Blessed are the meek for they shall inherit the earth.

JEWEL
Topaz

SEASON
Summer

RUTH

The Gleaner

The scene is laid in Bethlehem of Judea, which is situated some six miles south of Jerusalem, and also in Moab beyond the Jordan, bordering on and east of the Dead Sea. During the reign of the Judges a grievous famine spread throughout the land of Judah. Elimelich, his wife Naomi, and their two sons, Maholon and Chilton, determined to immigrate into the country of Moab beyond the Jordan Rover. There seems to have been no absolute necessity for this sojourn. Others continued to remain in Judea and tided over the period of distress.

While it would seem that upon their arrival in Moab they were well received by Eglon, the King of Moab, yet they did not prosper. The two sons married daughters of Moab. Mahlon, the eldest son, married Ruth (some writers say that Ruth was the young daughter of King Eglon), and Chilton married Orphah. Both women appear to have been model wives. Within ten years, however, Elimelech and his two sons died childless, and were buried in the land of Moab. Noami was left in destitute circumstances. Her heart and her spirit were broken. She felt that God had deserted her - the last link which bound her to earth was torn away. "The heart knows it sown bitterness." Thus, apparently, she is alone. What does the human heart dread more that to be utterly alone! Loneliness, how can we define it? One must experience it to know its real depth. "Kings and priest, warrior and maiden, philosopher and child - all must walk those might galleries alone." Naomi yearned for her old home and the home friends and resolved to return to Bethlehem again.

This story is the classic example of true and tried friendship between two women. It is often compared with David and Jonathan, and Damon and Pythias. It is the passionate love of a girl for her mother-in-law.

Definition of Gleaner:

1. vt accumulate something: to obtain information in small amounts over a period of time
2. vti agriculture gather after harvest: to go over a field or area that has just been harvested and gather by hand any usable parts of the crop that remain

Encarta ® World English Dictionary© & (P) 1998-2004 Microsoft Corporation. All rights reserved.

Color: The color appropriate to the degree is YELLOW, which symbolizes the ripened grain in the field of Boaz, in which Ruth was an humble gleaner.

Badge:

Sister Ruth, the badge of your office is the Sheaf with in the Triangle, symbolic of the abundance, which is the reward of diligence. The sheaf is an emblem of plenty, which, from its distinct and minute parts, teaches us that by patient industry, gleaning here a little and there a little, we may accumulate a competency to support us when the infirmities of age unfit us for the fatigues of labor.

Sign of the Widow:

Let the hands hang perpendicularly at the sides. Then raise them and hold them out horizontally forward, the elbows pressing against the sides of the body, as if showing the barley straw.

Bring the hands nearly side by side on the breast, a little way under the chin, letting the heads of the barley straw fall gracefully over the shoulders.

Cast the eyes upward.

Pass:

"Who is this?" A member n seeing the Widow's Sign should respond with these words.

Naomi Loses Her Husband and Sons

1 In the days when the judges ruled,[a] there was a famine in the land. So a man from Bethlehem in Judah, together with his wife and two sons, went to live for a while in the country of Moab. ²The man's name was Elimelek, his wife's name was Naomi, and the names of his two sons were Mahlon and Kilion. They were Ephrathites from Bethlehem, Judah. And they went to Moab and lived there.

³Now Elimelek, Naomi's husband, died, and she was left with her two sons. ⁴They married Moabite women, one named Orpah and the other Ruth. After they had lived there about ten years, ⁵both Mahlon and Kilion also died, and Naomi was left without her two sons and her husband.

Naomi and Ruth Return to Bethlehem

⁶When Naomi heard in Moab that the LORD had come to the aid of his people by providing food for them, she and her daughters-in-law prepared to return home from there. ⁷With her two daughters-in-law she left the place where she had been living and set out on the road that would take them back to the land of Judah.

⁸Then Naomi said to her two daughters-in-law, "Go back, each of you, to your mother's home. May the LORD show you kindness, as you have shown kindness to your dead husbands and to me. ⁹May the LORD grant that each of you will find rest in the home of another husband."

Then she kissed them goodbye and they wept aloud ¹⁰and said to her, "We will go back with you to your people."

¹¹But Naomi said, "Return home, my daughters. Why would you come with me? Am I going to have any more sons, who could become your husbands? ¹²Return home, my daughters; I am too old to have another husband. Even if I thought there was still hope for me—even if I had a husband tonight and then gave birth to sons— ¹³would you wait until they grew up? Would you remain unmarried for them? No, my daughters. It is

more bitter for me than for you, because the Lord's hand has turned against me!"

¹⁴At this they wept aloud again. Then Orpah kissed her mother-in-law goodbye, but Ruth clung to her.

¹⁵"Look," said Naomi, "your sister-in-law is going back to her people and her gods. Go back with her."

¹⁶But Ruth replied, "Don't urge me to leave you or to turn back from you. Where you go I will go, and where you stay I will stay. Your people will be my people and your God my God. ¹⁷Where you die I will die, and there I will be buried. May the Lord deal with me, be it ever so severely, if even death separates you and me." ¹⁸When Naomi realized that Ruth was determined to go with her, she stopped urging her.

¹⁹So the two women went on until they came to Bethlehem. When they arrived in Bethlehem, the whole town was stirred because of them, and the women exclaimed, "Can this be Naomi?"

²⁰"Don't call me Naomi,ᵃ" she told them. "Call me Mara,ᵇ because the Almightyᶜ has made my life very bitter. ²¹I went away full, but the Lord has brought me back empty. Why call me Naomi? The Lord has afflictedᵈ me; the Almighty has brought misfortune upon me."

²²So Naomi returned from Moab accompanied by Ruth the Moabite, her daughter-in-law, arriving in Bethlehem as the barley harvest was beginning.

69

Ruth Meets Boaz in the Grain Field

2 Now Naomi had a relative on her husband's side, a man of standing from the clan of Elimelek, whose name was Boaz.

² And Ruth the Moabite said to Naomi, "Let me go to the fields and pick up the leftover grain behind anyone in whose eyes I find favor."

Naomi said to her, "Go ahead, my daughter." ³ So she went out, entered a field and began to glean behind the harvesters. As it turned out, she was working in a field belonging to Boaz, who was from the clan of Elimelek.

⁴ Just then Boaz arrived from Bethlehem and greeted the harvesters, "The LORD be with you!"

"The LORD bless you!" they answered.

⁵ Boaz asked the overseer of his harvesters, "Who does that young woman belong to?"

⁶ The overseer replied, "She is the Moabite who came back from Moab with Naomi. ⁷ She said, 'Please let me glean and gather among the sheaves behind the harvesters.' She came into the field and has remained here from morning till now, except for a short rest in the shelter."

⁸ So Boaz said to Ruth, "My daughter, listen to me. Don't go and glean in another field and don't go away from here. Stay here with the women who work for me. ⁹ Watch the field where the men are harvesting, and follow along after the women. I have told the men not to lay a hand on you. And whenever you are thirsty, go and get a drink from the water jars the men have filled."

¹⁰ At this, she bowed down with her face to the ground. She asked him, "Why have I found such favor in your eyes that you notice me—a foreigner?"

¹¹ Boaz replied, "I've been told all about what you have done for your mother-in-law since the death of your husband—how you left your father and mother and your homeland and came to live with a people you did not know before. ¹² May the LORD repay you for what you have done. May you be

richly rewarded by the LORD, the God of Israel, under whose wings you have come to take refuge."

[13]"May I continue to find favor in your eyes, my lord," she said. "You have put me at ease by speaking kindly to your servant—though I do not have the standing of one of your servants."

[14]At mealtime Boaz said to her, "Come over here. Have some bread and dip it in the wine vinegar."

When she sat down with the harvesters, he offered her some roasted grain. She ate all she wanted and had some left over. [15]As she got up to glean, Boaz gave orders to his men, "Let her gather among the sheaves and don't reprimand her. [16]Even pull out some stalks for her from the bundles and leave them for her to pick up, and don't rebuke her."

[17]So Ruth gleaned in the field until evening. Then she threshed the barley she had gathered, and it amounted to about an ephah.[a] [18]She carried it back to town, and her mother-in-law saw how much she had gathered. Ruth also brought out and gave her what she had left over after she had eaten enough.

[19]Her mother-in-law asked her, "Where did you glean today? Where did you work? Blessed be the man who took notice of you!"

Then Ruth told her mother-in-law about the one at whose place she had been working. "The name of the man I worked with today is Boaz," she said.

[20]"The LORD bless him!" Naomi said to her daughter-in-law. "He has not stopped showing his kindness to the living and the dead." She added, "That man is our close relative; he is one of our guardian-redeemers.[b]"

[21]Then Ruth the Moabite said, "He even said to me, 'Stay with my workers until they finish harvesting all my grain.'"

[22]Naomi said to Ruth her daughter-in-law, "It will be good for you, my daughter, to go with the women who work for him, because in someone else's field you might be harmed."

[23]So Ruth stayed close to the women of Boaz to glean until the barley and wheat harvests were finished. And she lived with her mother-in-law.

Ruth and Boaz at the Threshing Floor

3 One day Ruth's mother-in-law Naomi said to her, "My daughter, I must find a home[a] for you, where you will be well provided for. ²Now Boaz, with whose women you have worked, is a relative of ours. Tonight he will be winnowing barley on the threshing floor. ³Wash, put on perfume, and get dressed in your best clothes. Then go down to the threshing floor, but don't let him know you are there until he has finished eating and drinking. ⁴When he lies down, note the place where he is lying. Then go and uncover his feet and lie down. He will tell you what to do."

⁵"I will do whatever you say," Ruth answered. ⁶So she went down to the threshing floor and did everything her mother-in-law told her to do.

⁷When Boaz had finished eating and drinking and was in good spirits, he went over to lie down at the far end of the grain pile. Ruth approached quietly, uncovered his feet and lay down. ⁸In the middle of the night something startled the man; he turned—and there was a woman lying at his feet!

⁹"Who are you?" he asked.

"I am your servant Ruth," she said. "Spread the corner of your garment over me, since you are a guardian-redeemer[b] of our family."

¹⁰"The LORD bless you, my daughter," he replied. "This kindness is greater than that which you showed earlier: You have not run after the younger men, whether rich or poor. ¹¹And now, my daughter, don't be afraid. I will do for you all you ask. All the people of my town know that you are a woman of noble character. ¹²Although it is true that I am a guardian-redeemer of our family, there is another who is more closely related than I. ¹³Stay here for the night, and in the morning if he wants to do his duty as your guardian-redeemer, good; let him redeem you. But if he is not willing, as surely as the LORD lives I will do it. Lie here until morning."

¹⁴So she lay at his feet until morning, but got up before anyone could be recognized; and he said, "No one must know that a woman came to the threshing floor."

¹⁵He also said, "Bring me the shawl you are wearing and hold it out." When she did so, he poured into it six measures of barley and placed the bundle on her. Then heᵗᵈ went back to town.

¹⁶When Ruth came to her mother-in-law, Naomi asked, "How did it go, my daughter?"

Then she told her everything Boaz had done for her ¹⁷and added, "He gave me these six measures of barley, saying, 'Don't go back to your mother-in-law empty-handed.'"

¹⁸Then Naomi said, "Wait, my daughter, until you find out what happens. For the man will not rest until the matter is settled today."

Boaz Marries Ruth

4 Meanwhile Boaz went up to the town gate and sat down there just as the guardian-redeemer[a] he had mentioned came along. Boaz said, "Come over here, my friend, and sit down." So he went over and sat down.

2 Boaz took ten of the elders of the town and said, "Sit here," and they did so. 3 Then he said to the guardian-redeemer, "Naomi, who has come back from Moab, is selling the piece of land that belonged to our relative Elimelek. 4 I thought I should bring the matter to your attention and suggest that you buy it in the presence of these seated here and in the presence of the elders of my people. If you will redeem it, do so. But if you[b] will not, tell me, so I will know. For no one has the right to do it except you, and I am next in line."

"I will redeem it," he said.

5 Then Boaz said, "On the day you buy the land from Naomi, you also acquire Ruth the Moabite, the[c] dead man's widow, in order to maintain the name of the dead with his property."

6 At this, the guardian-redeemer said, "Then I cannot redeem it because I might endanger my own estate. You redeem it yourself. I cannot do it."

7 (Now in earlier times in Israel, for the redemption and transfer of property to become final, one party took off his sandal and gave it to the other. This was the method of legalizing transactions in Israel.)

8 So the guardian-redeemer said to Boaz, "Buy it yourself." And he removed his sandal.

9 Then Boaz announced to the elders and all the people, "Today you are witnesses that I have bought from Naomi all the property of Elimelek, Kilion and Mahlon. 10 I have also acquired Ruth the Moabite, Mahlon's widow, as my wife, in order to maintain the name of the dead with his property, so that his name will not disappear from among his family or from his hometown. Today you are witnesses!"

[11]Then the elders and all the people at the gate said, "We are witnesses. May the LORD make the woman who is coming into your home like Rachel and Leah, who together built up the family of Israel. May you have standing in Ephrathah and be famous in Bethlehem. [12]Through the offspring the LORD gives you by this young woman, may your family be like that of Perez, whom Tamar bore to Judah."

Naomi Gains a Son

[13]So Boaz took Ruth and she became his wife. When he made love to her, the LORD enabled her to conceive, and she gave birth to a son. [14]The women said to Naomi: "Praise be to the LORD, who this day has not left you without a guardian-redeemer. May he become famous throughout Israel! [15]He will renew your life and sustain you in your old age. For your daughter-in-law, who loves you and who is better to you than seven sons, has given him birth."

[16]Then Naomi took the child in her arms and cared for him. [17]The women living there said, "Naomi has a son!" And they named him Obed. He was the father of Jesse, the father of David.

The Genealogy of David

[18]This, then, is the family line of Perez:

Perez was the father of Hezron,

[19]Hezron the father of Ram,

Ram the father of Amminadab,

[20]Amminadab the father of Nahshon,

Nahshon the father of Salmon,[c]

[21]Salmon the father of Boaz,

Boaz the father of Obed,

[22]Obed the father of Jesse,

and Jesse the father of David.

Ruth 1 King James Version (KJV)

1 Now it came to pass in the days when the judges ruled, that there was a famine in the land. And a certain man of Bethlehemjudah went to sojourn in the country of Moab, he, and his wife, and his two sons.

2 And the name of the man was Elimelech, and the name of his wife Naomi, and the name of his two sons Mahlon and Chilion, Ephrathites of Bethlehemjudah. And they came into the country of Moab, and continued there.

3 And Elimelech Naomi's husband died; and she was left, and her two sons.

4 And they took them wives of the women of Moab; the name of the one was Orpah, and the name of the other Ruth: and they dwelled there about ten years.

5 And Mahlon and Chilion died also both of them; and the woman was left of her two sons and her husband.

6 Then she arose with her daughters in law, that she might return from the country of Moab: for she had heard in the country of Moab how that the LORD had visited his people in giving them bread.

7 Wherefore she went forth out of the place where she was, and her two daughters in law with her; and they went on the way to return unto the land of Judah.

8 And Naomi said unto her two daughters in law, Go, return each to her mother's house: the LORD deal kindly with you, as ye have dealt with the dead, and with me.

9 The LORD grant you that ye may find rest, each of you in the house of her husband. Then she kissed them; and they lifted up their voice, and wept.

10 And they said unto her, Surely we will return with thee unto thy people.

11 And Naomi said, Turn again, my daughters: why will ye go with me? are there yet any more sons in my womb, that they may be your husbands?

12 Turn again, my daughters, go your way; for I am too old to have an husband. If I should say, I have hope, if I should have an husband also to night, and should also bear sons;

¹³Would ye tarry for them till they were grown? would ye stay for them from having husbands? nay, my daughters; for it grieveth me much for your sakes that the hand of the LORD is gone out against me.

¹⁴And they lifted up their voice, and wept again: and Orpah kissed her mother in law; but Ruth clave unto her.

¹⁵And she said, Behold, thy sister in law is gone back unto her people, and unto her gods: return thou after thy sister in law.

¹⁶And Ruth said, Intreat me not to leave thee, or to return from following after thee: for whither thou goest, I will go; and where thou lodgest, I will lodge: thy people shall be my people, and thy God my God:

¹⁷Where thou diest, will I die, and there will I be buried: the LORD do so to me, and more also, if ought but death part thee and me.

¹⁸When she saw that she was stedfastly minded to go with her, then she left speaking unto her.

¹⁹So they two went until they came to Bethlehem. And it came to pass, when they were come to Bethlehem, that all the city was moved about them, and they said, Is this Naomi?

²⁰And she said unto them, Call me not Naomi, call me Mara: for the Almighty hath dealt very bitterly with me.

²¹I went out full and the LORD hath brought me home again empty: why then call ye me Naomi, seeing the LORD hath testified against me, and the Almighty hath afflicted me?

²²So Naomi returned, and Ruth the Moabitess, her daughter in law, with her, which returned out of the country of Moab: and they came to Bethlehem in the beginning of barley harvest.

2 And Naomi had a kinsman of her husband's, a mighty man of wealth, of the family of Elimelech; and his name was Boaz.

2And Ruth the Moabitess said unto Naomi, Let me now go to the field, and glean ears of corn after him in whose sight I shall find grace. And she said unto her, Go, my daughter.

3And she went, and came, and gleaned in the field after the reapers: and her hap was to light on a part of the field belonging unto Boaz, who was of the kindred of Elimelech.

4And, behold, Boaz came from Bethlehem, and said unto the reapers, The LORD be with you. And they answered him, The LORD bless thee.

5Then said Boaz unto his servant that was set over the reapers, Whose damsel is this?

6And the servant that was set over the reapers answered and said, It is the Moabitish damsel that came back with Naomi out of the country of Moab:

7And she said, I pray you, let me glean and gather after the reapers among the sheaves: so she came, and hath continued even from the morning until now, that she tarried a little in the house.

8Then said Boaz unto Ruth, Hearest thou not, my daughter? Go not to glean in another field, neither go from hence, but abide here fast by my maidens:

9Let thine eyes be on the field that they do reap, and go thou after them: have I not charged the young men that they shall not touch thee? and when thou art athirst, go unto the vessels, and drink of that which the young men have drawn.

10Then she fell on her face, and bowed herself to the ground, and said unto him, Why have I found grace in thine eyes, that thou shouldest take knowledge of me, seeing I am a stranger?

11And Boaz answered and said unto her, It hath fully been shewed me, all that thou hast done unto thy mother in law since the death of thine husband: and how thou hast left thy father and thy mother, and the land of thy nativity, and art come unto a people which thou knewest not heretofore.

¹²The LORD recompense thy work, and a full reward be given thee of the LORD God of Israel, under whose wings thou art come to trust.

¹³Then she said, Let me find favour in thy sight, my lord; for that thou hast comforted me, and for that thou hast spoken friendly unto thine handmaid, though I be not like unto one of thine handmaidens.

¹⁴And Boaz said unto her, At mealtime come thou hither, and eat of the bread, and dip thy morsel in the vinegar. And she sat beside the reapers: and he reached her parched corn, and she did eat, and was sufficed, and left.

¹⁵And when she was risen up to glean, Boaz commanded his young men, saying, Let her glean even among the sheaves, and reproach her not:

¹⁶And let fall also some of the handfuls of purpose for her, and leave them, that she may glean them, and rebuke her not.

¹⁷So she gleaned in the field until even, and beat out that she had gleaned: and it was about an ephah of barley.

¹⁸And she took it up, and went into the city: and her mother in law saw what she had gleaned: and she brought forth, and gave to her that she had reserved after she was sufficed.

¹⁹And her mother in law said unto her, Where hast thou gleaned to day? and where wroughtest thou? blessed be he that did take knowledge of thee. And she shewed her mother in law with whom she had wrought, and said, The man's name with whom I wrought to day is Boaz.

²⁰And Naomi said unto her daughter in law, Blessed be he of the LORD, who hath not left off his kindness to the living and to the dead. And Naomi said unto her, The man is near of kin unto us, one of our next kinsmen.

²¹And Ruth the Moabitess said, He said unto me also, Thou shalt keep fast by my young men, until they have ended all my harvest.

²²And Naomi said unto Ruth her daughter in law, It is good, my daughter, that thou go out with his maidens, that they meet thee not in any other field.

[23] So she kept fast by the maidens of Boaz to glean unto the end of barley harvest and of wheat harvest; and dwelt with her mother in law.

Ruth 3 King James Version (KJV)

3 Then Naomi her mother in law said unto her, My daughter, shall I not seek rest for thee, that it may be well with thee?

²And now is not Boaz of our kindred, with whose maidens thou wast? Behold, he winnoweth barley to night in the threshingfloor.

³Wash thyself therefore, and anoint thee, and put thy raiment upon thee, and get thee down to the floor: but make not thyself known unto the man, until he shall have done eating and drinking.

⁴And it shall be, when he lieth down, that thou shalt mark the place where he shall lie, and thou shalt go in, and uncover his feet, and lay thee down; and he will tell thee what thou shalt do.

⁵And she said unto her, All that thou sayest unto me I will do.

⁶And she went down unto the floor, and did according to all that her mother in law bade her.

⁷And when Boaz had eaten and drunk, and his heart was merry, he went to lie down at the end of the heap of corn: and she came softly, and uncovered his feet, and laid her down.

⁸And it came to pass at midnight, that the man was afraid, and turned himself: and, behold, a woman lay at his feet.

⁹And he said, Who art thou? And she answered, I am Ruth thine handmaid: spread therefore thy skirt over thine handmaid; for thou art a near kinsman.

¹⁰And he said, Blessed be thou of the LORD, my daughter: for thou hast shewed more kindness in the latter end than at the beginning, inasmuch as thou followedst not young men, whether poor or rich.

¹¹And now, my daughter, fear not; I will do to thee all that thou requirest: for all the city of my people doth know that thou art a virtuous woman.

¹²And now it is true that I am thy near kinsman: howbeit there is a kinsman nearer than I.

¹³Tarry this night, and it shall be in the morning, that if he will perform unto thee the part of a kinsman, well; let him do the kinsman's part: but if he will

not do the part of a kinsman to thee, then will I do the part of a kinsman to thee, as the LORD liveth: lie down until the morning.

¹⁴And she lay at his feet until the morning: and she rose up before one could know another. And he said, Let it not be known that a woman came into the floor.

¹⁵Also he said, Bring the vail that thou hast upon thee, and hold it. And when she held it, he measured six measures of barley, and laid it on her: and she went into the city.

¹⁶And when she came to her mother in law, she said, Who art thou, my daughter? And she told her all that the man had done to her.

¹⁷And she said, These six measures of barley gave he me; for he said to me, Go not empty unto thy mother in law.

¹⁸Then said she, Sit still, my daughter, until thou know how the matter will fall: for the man will not be in rest, until he have finished the thing this day.

Ruth 4 King James Version (KJV)

4 Then went Boaz up to the gate, and sat him down there: and, behold, the kinsman of whom Boaz spake came by; unto whom he said, Ho, such a one! turn aside, sit down here. And he turned aside, and sat down.

²And he took ten men of the elders of the city, and said, Sit ye down here. And they sat down.

³And he said unto the kinsman, Naomi, that is come again out of the country of Moab, selleth a parcel of land, which was our brother Elimelech's:

⁴And I thought to advertise thee, saying, Buy it before the inhabitants, and before the elders of my people. If thou wilt redeem it, redeem it: but if thou wilt not redeem it, then tell me, that I may know: for there is none to redeem it beside thee; and I am after thee. And he said, I will redeem it.

⁵Then said Boaz, What day thou buyest the field of the hand of Naomi, thou must buy it also of Ruth the Moabitess, the wife of the dead, to raise up the name of the dead upon his inheritance.

⁶And the kinsman said, I cannot redeem it for myself, lest I mar mine own inheritance: redeem thou my right to thyself; for I cannot redeem it.

⁷Now this was the manner in former time in Israel concerning redeeming and concerning changing, for to confirm all things; a man plucked off his shoe, and gave it to his neighbour: and this was a testimony in Israel.

⁸Therefore the kinsman said unto Boaz, Buy it for thee. So he drew off his shoe.

⁹And Boaz said unto the elders, and unto all the people, Ye are witnesses this day, that I have bought all that was Elimelech's, and all that was Chilion's and Mahlon's, of the hand of Naomi.

¹⁰Moreover Ruth the Moabitess, the wife of Mahlon, have I purchased to be my wife, to raise up the name of the dead upon his inheritance, that the name of the dead be not cut off from among his brethren, and from the gate of his place: ye are witnesses this day.

¹¹And all the people that were in the gate, and the elders, said, We are witnesses. The LORD make the woman that is come into thine house like

Rachel and like Leah, which two did build the house of Israel: and do thou worthily in Ephratah, and be famous in Bethlehem:

¹²And let thy house be like the house of Pharez, whom Tamar bare unto Judah, of the seed which the Lord shall give thee of this young woman.

¹³So Boaz took Ruth, and she was his wife: and when he went in unto her, the Lord gave her conception, and she bare a son.

¹⁴And the women said unto Naomi, Blessed be the Lord, which hath not left thee this day without a kinsman, that his name may be famous in Israel.

¹⁵And he shall be unto thee a restorer of thy life, and a nourisher of thine old age: for thy daughter in law, which loveth thee, which is better to thee than seven sons, hath born him.

¹⁶And Naomi took the child, and laid it in her bosom, and became nurse unto it.

¹⁷And the women her neighbours gave it a name, saying, There is a son born to Naomi; and they called his name Obed: he is the father of Jesse, the father of David.

¹⁸Now these are the generations of Pharez: Pharez begat Hezron,

¹⁹And Hezron begat Ram, and Ram begat Amminadab,

²⁰And Amminadab begat Nahshon, and Nahshon begat Salmon,

²¹And Salmon begat Boaz, and Boaz begat Obed,

²²And Obed begat Jesse, and Jesse begat David.

QUESTION	ANSWER
What does the name RUTH stand for?	A Friend
Why did Ruth leave home?	She was following Naomi.
Where was Ruth's original home?	The land of Moab.
Ruth was a descendent of whom?	Lot.
What did Ruth do for a living in her new home?	She gleaned in the fields.
How did Ruth meet Boaz?	While she was gleaning in his field.
How was the marriage of Ruth and Boaz made possible?	Through the Israelites custom exchange of a shoe (Ruth 4:7-8)
For what will Ruth always be remembered?	For being the mother of the ancestral line of Christ.
What does the story of Ruth teach us?	It teaches that we may have to give up our most cherished things to become a true friend.
What does the color yellow symbolize?	Sincere affection and that which is divine.
What does the Sheaf of Grain teach us?	It teaches that we may have to give up our most cherished things to become a true friend.
What is the original flower dedicated to Ruth?	The sunflower.
What flower at present is dedicated to Ruth?	The Yellow Jasmine
What is Ruth's jewel?	The Topaz.
Where did Ruth spend her early life?	In the City of Bethlehem.
Who is Oprah?	Naomi's other daughter-in-law.
Naomi told her friends in Bethlehem to call her what?	Mara, which means bitter.
What do the historical periods of the stories of Ruth and Adah have in common?	They both occurred during the time Israel was ruled by Judges.
What was Naomi's Husband's name?	Elimelech
What does the name Naomi mean?	God in sweetness.
Who were the Moabites?	The descendants of Lot.
Who was Boaz?	A wealthy farmer, the son of Rahab, and a cousin of Naomi's husband.
Were any children born Ruth and Boaz?	Yes, Obed, the grandfather of David.
What was the name of Ruth's first husband?	Mahlon

Ruth is the second Star Point Heroine

Ruth represents the ideal Widow because she cherished the family, faith and inheritance of her husband above every personal ambition, her original native allegiance, and her originally heathen religion.

The name "RUTH" means "FRIEND". Ruth's allegiance to her mother-in-law was maintained only through Ruth's ability to sacrifice herself for the sake of another. Her friendship with Naomi has become one of the world's greatest examples of the true meaning of friendship.

Yellow represents "constancy", "exalted", and "richness" and it is dedicated to Ruth. Ruth was characterized by a radiant and strong personality and it is therefore that the color of the sun, "exalted in the heavens," is dedicated to her. Her position in the ancestral line of the Christ is sufficient testimony to the richness of her own personal worth.

The Yellow Jasmine is dedicated to her because it has an associated meaning of "humbleness". This is a fitting tribute to Ruth who was willing to do the most humble type of work for the sake of Naomi.

The ideals of the Second Star Point are Loyalty and Friendship. If we would become the ideal friend to another or, if we would like to be the recipient of a mother's friendship, we must first be deserving.

The sheaf is the emblem of Ruth, it represents the collective worth of many small deeds of kindness which are done for the sake of a mother.

The Lily of the Valley is the symbol of the larger concept of Ruth. As Christ, the Lily of the Valley, left his heavenly home and His Father to serve humankind on earth, so Ruth left her home and people to serve her fellow man, Naomi, in a strange and unfamiliar country.

The story of Ruth challenges us to serve our fellow man and to extend the hand of friendship to all who may have need.

The yellow Topaz has been dedicated to Ruth. This jewel has been associated with "rarity". Certainly a friendship shared and enjoyed by Ruth and Naomi was a rare gem and well worth treasuring.

Ruth represents the summer season, and, symbolically, the growing maturing season of life itself. Ruth represents that period in human life when the peak of one's capacity is achieved and the individual has the mental, emotional and physical stability to make the greatest strides in shaping of earthly life.

The third Beatitude is associated with Ruth. "Blessed are the meek for they shall inherit the earth." Matthew 5:5

Book of Ruth

The Book of Ruth, considered one of the finest pieces of literature ever written, has its primary purpose that of establishing the line of the House of David and of Jesus Christ. After the death of Naomi's, Ruth's, and Orpah's husbands, Naomi decided to return to her homeland. Ruth's willingness to become a foreigner, as well as her devotion and concern for Naomi was proof of love and friendship. Ruth, a Moabite who had been denied even admission into the Hebrew congregation by every law and tradition, became part of the ancestral line of Christ.

Read the Book of Ruth

Complied by Alberta W. Jones, G.M.

Story of Esther

Esther

Definition	A Star
Degree	Wife
Gem	Diamond
Flower	Lily of the Valley
Teaching	Pure
Emblem	Crown and Scepter
Color	White
	(Pure, Hope, & Light)
Beatitude	7th Beatitude (Matthew 5:9)
Verse Reference	Book of Esther
Song	Shine on Me
Season	None
Pass	What Will Thou

ESTHER

3rd POINT OF THE STAR

Degree	Wife
Meaning	Star
Color	White
Flower	White Lily
Emblem	Crown & Scepter
Symbol	Sun

PASS
What wilt thou?

BEATITUDE
Blessed are the peacemakers for they shall be called the children of GOD.

JEWEL
Diamond

SEASON

ESTHER

The Nobel Queen
The Crown and Scepter of Esther

Robert Morris recognized Loyalty as one of the most important virtues for us all to strive for in life, and so he included it as one of the lessons in our Ritual. Queen Esther and her life were chosen as an example of Loyalty to friends, to country, to God.

To more firmly impress this on our minds, he chose a Crown and Scepter as the symbol of Esther's station because she was a Queen who portrayed these virtues at great personal risk. The Scepter denotes the power and authority of the King but it also clearly illustrates the self-discipline of Esther as she strictly observed the rules of the Court in order to obtain an audience with the King.

ESTHER (es'tuhr) HEBREW: ESTER "star"

The Jewish wife of King Ahasuerus of Persia (know to history as Xerxes I, 485-586 B.C.), Esther is the heroine of the biblical book bearing her name, a work that is considered one of the masterpieces of storytelling in ancient world literature.

Esther's Jewish name was Hadassah, the Hebrew word for myrtle. Born in Susa, the former capital of Elam, which had been absorbed by Persia, she was orphaned at an early age and brought up by an older cousin named Mordecai His family had been taken captive from Judah years earlier, after the fall of Jerusalem to Nebuchadnezzar in 586 B. C.

After his wife Vashti embarrassed him by refusing to make a command appearance at a royal banquet, Ahasuerus ordered a search for a new queen to replace her. Esther, a maiden "beautiful and lovely" was among the many young women brought into the harem and put in the custody of the king's eunuch Hegai. But Mordecai continued to keep an eye on his ward - then know by her Persian name, Esther, from the word for .star - and charged her not to give away her Jewish identity. For a year Esther was trained in the arts of the harem, and when she finally made her first appearance before the king, he "loved Esther more than all the women, and she found grace and favor in his sight more than all the virgins" (Est. 2:17). Ahasuerus promptly named Esther his queen.

One day as Mordecai was lingering near the palace, he overheard two guards, discussing a plot to kill the king. Quickly, he passed the word to Esther, who told the king, and the two guards were hanged. Soon thereafter the king named Haman the Agagite as his grand vizier. When Mordecai alone among the spectators at the place gate refused to bow in obeisance as Haman rode by, the :furious grand vizier plotted the destruction not just of Mordecai but also of the entire Jewish population of the kingdom. To obtain an auspicious date for the pogrom to begin, he cast lots and came up with the 13th day of the 12th month, Adar.

When the terrible decree was published, Mordecai appealed to Esther to intervene with the king. She took the risk of appearing unsummoned before the king, but was warmly received and told that any request she made would be granted. She first asked the king to invite Haman to the banquet she was giving that evening. Haman accepted, enjoyed himself: and was invited to another banquet the following evening. His elation at this newfound favor with the queen was ruined when he again met an unrepentant Mordecai at the palace gate.

Ignoring his previous announcement of the date for killing the Jews, Haman decided to go after Mordecai at once. He ordered a huge gallows built and went to the palace to obtain permission to hang Mordecai on it Coincidentally, however, the king was having trouble sleeping and had asked that the royal journal be read to him. Foruitously, he learned how Mordecai had earlier saved his life and realized that he had never been rewarded. When Haman appeared, the king asked his advice; "What should be done to the man whom the king delights to honor?" (Est. 6:6). Smugly assuming that the king meant him. Haman suggested a royal procession in his honor. The king then ordered Haman to "do so to Mordecai the Hew who sits at the king's gate" (Est. 6:10)

That evening after the second dinner with Haman, Esther revealed her Jewish identity, and then told of the plot to kill her people, climactically pointing out Haman as the person behind the murderous scheme, enraged, the king stalked from the room to consider an appropriate fate for Haman. Throwing himself at the queen's feet, the terrified grand vizer made a pathetic appeal to Esther for his life. The king returned to the room, thought Haman was attacking the queen, and ordered him taken out and hanged immediately - on the very gallows he had built for Mordecai. The king rewarded Esther with al of Haman's estate, bestowed Haman's signet ring on Mordecai, grand vizier, and revoked Haman's edicts against the Jews.

On the day chosen by Haman for their deaths, the Jews of Persia took their revenge, slaying their enemies in Susa and throughout the land. The next day, the 14th became a day of festivities, one still celebrated as Purim, in ironic reference to the twist of fate dealt the Jews by Haman's casting of lots.

Esther 1 New International Version (NIV)

Queen Vashti Deposed

1 This is what happened during the time of Xerxes,[a] the Xerxes who ruled over 127 provinces stretching from India to Cush[b]: ²At that time King Xerxes reigned from his royal throne in the citadel of Susa, ³and in the third year of his reign he gave a banquet for all his nobles and officials. The military leaders of Persia and Media, the princes, and the nobles of the provinces were present.

⁴For a full 180 days he displayed the vast wealth of his kingdom and the splendor and glory of his majesty. ⁵When these days were over, the king gave a banquet, lasting seven days, in the enclosed garden of the king's palace, for all the people from the least to the greatest who were in the citadel of Susa. ⁶The garden had hangings of white and blue linen, fastened with cords of white linen and purple material to silver rings on marble pillars. There were couches of gold and silver on a mosaic pavement of porphyry, marble, mother-of-pearl and other costly stones. ⁷Wine was served in goblets of gold, each one different from the other, and the royal wine was abundant, in keeping with the king's liberality. ⁸By the king's command each guest was allowed to drink with no restrictions, for the king instructed all the wine stewards to serve each man what he wished.

⁹Queen Vashti also gave a banquet for the women in the royal palace of King Xerxes.

¹⁰On the seventh day, when King Xerxes was in high spirits from wine, he commanded the seven eunuchs who served him—Mehuman, Biztha, Harbona, Bigtha, Abagtha, Zethar and Karkas— ¹¹to bring before him Queen Vashti, wearing her royal crown, in order to display her beauty to the people and nobles, for she was lovely to look at. ¹²But when the attendants delivered the king's command, Queen Vashti refused to come. Then the king became furious and burned with anger.

¹³Since it was customary for the king to consult experts in matters of law and justice, he spoke with the wise men who understood the times ¹⁴and were closest to the king—Karshena, Shethar, Admatha, Tarshish, Meres, Marsena

and Memukan, the seven nobles of Persia and Media who had special access to the king and were highest in the kingdom.

¹⁵"According to law, what must be done to Queen Vashti?" he asked. "She has not obeyed the command of King Xerxes that the eunuchs have taken to her."

¹⁶Then Memukan replied in the presence of the king and the nobles, "Queen Vashti has done wrong, not only against the king but also against all the nobles and the peoples of all the provinces of King Xerxes. ¹⁷For the queen's conduct will become known to all the women, and so they will despise their husbands and say, 'King Xerxes commanded Queen Vashti to be brought before him, but she would not come.' ¹⁸This very day the Persian and Median women of the nobility who have heard about the queen's conduct will respond to all the king's nobles in the same way. There will be no end of disrespect and discord.

¹⁹"Therefore, if it pleases the king, let him issue a royal decree and let it be written in the laws of Persia and Media, which cannot be repealed, that Vashti is never again to enter the presence of King Xerxes. Also let the king give her royal position to someone else who is better than she. ²⁰Then when the king's edict is proclaimed throughout all his vast realm, all the women will respect their husbands, from the least to the greatest."

²¹The king and his nobles were pleased with this advice, so the king did as Memukan proposed. ²²He sent dispatches to all parts of the kingdom, to each province in its own script and to each people in their own language, proclaiming that every man should be ruler over his own household, using his native tongue.

Esther Made Queen

2 Later when King Xerxes' fury had subsided, he remembered Vashti and what she had done and what he had decreed about her. ²Then the king's personal attendants proposed, "Let a search be made for beautiful young virgins for the king. ³Let the king appoint commissioners in every province of his realm to bring all these beautiful young women into the harem at the citadel of Susa. Let them be placed under the care of Hegai, the king's eunuch, who is in charge of the women; and let beauty treatments be given to them. ⁴Then let the young woman who pleases the king be queen instead of Vashti." This advice appealed to the king, and he followed it.

⁵Now there was in the citadel of Susa a Jew of the tribe of Benjamin, named Mordecai son of Jair, the son of Shimei, the son of Kish, ⁶who had been carried into exile from Jerusalem by Nebuchadnezzar king of Babylon, among those taken captive with Jehoiachin king of Judah. ⁷Mordecai had a cousin named Hadassah, whom he had brought up because she had neither father nor mother. This young woman, who was also known as Esther, had a lovely figure and was beautiful. Mordecai had taken her as his own daughter when her father and mother died.

⁸When the king's order and edict had been proclaimed, many young women were brought to the citadel of Susa and put under the care of Hegai. Esther also was taken to the king's palace and entrusted to Hegai, who had charge of the harem. ⁹She pleased him and won his favor. Immediately he provided her with her beauty treatments and special food. He assigned to her seven female attendants selected from the king's palace and moved her and her attendants into the best place in the harem.

¹⁰Esther had not revealed her nationality and family background, because Mordecai had forbidden her to do so. ¹¹Every day he walked back and forth near the courtyard of the harem to find out how Esther was and what was happening to her.

¹²Before a young woman's turn came to go in to King Xerxes, she had to complete twelve months of beauty treatments prescribed for the women, six

months with oil of myrrh and six with perfumes and cosmetics. ¹³And this is how she would go to the king: Anything she wanted was given her to take with her from the harem to the king's palace. ¹⁴In the evening she would go there and in the morning return to another part of the harem to the care of Shaashgaz, the king's eunuch who was in charge of the concubines. She would not return to the king unless he was pleased with her and summoned her by name.

¹⁵When the turn came for Esther (the young woman Mordecai had adopted, the daughter of his uncle Abihail) to go to the king, she asked for nothing other than what Hegai, the king's eunuch who was in charge of the harem, suggested. And Esther won the favor of everyone who saw her. ¹⁶She was taken to King Xerxes in the royal residence in the tenth month, the month of Tebeth, in the seventh year of his reign.

¹⁷Now the king was attracted to Esther more than to any of the other women, and she won his favor and approval more than any of the other virgins. So he set a royal crown on her head and made her queen instead of Vashti. ¹⁸And the king gave a great banquet, Esther's banquet, for all his nobles and officials. He proclaimed a holiday throughout the provinces and distributed gifts with royal liberality.

Mordecai Uncovers a Conspiracy

¹⁹When the virgins were assembled a second time, Mordecai was sitting at the king's gate. ²⁰But Esther had kept secret her family background and nationality just as Mordecai had told her to do, for she continued to follow Mordecai's instructions as she had done when he was bringing her up.

²¹During the time Mordecai was sitting at the king's gate, Bigthana and Teresh, two of the king's officers who guarded the doorway, became angry and conspired to assassinate King Xerxes. ²²But Mordecai found out about the plot and told Queen Esther, who in turn reported it to the king, giving credit to Mordecai. ²³And when the report was investigated and found to be true, the two officials were impaled on poles. All this was recorded in the book of the annals in the presence of the king.

Esther 3 New International Version (NIV)

Haman's Plot to Destroy the Jews

3 After these events, King Xerxes honored Haman son of Hammedatha, the Agagite, elevating him and giving him a seat of honor higher than that of all the other nobles. ²All the royal officials at the king's gate knelt down and paid honor to Haman, for the king had commanded this concerning him. But Mordecai would not kneel down or pay him honor.

³Then the royal officials at the king's gate asked Mordecai, "Why do you disobey the king's command?" ⁴Day after day they spoke to him but he refused to comply. Therefore they told Haman about it to see whether Mordecai's behavior would be tolerated, for he had told them he was a Jew.

⁵When Haman saw that Mordecai would not kneel down or pay him honor, he was enraged. ⁶Yet having learned who Mordecai's people were, he scorned the idea of killing only Mordecai. Instead Haman looked for a way to destroy all Mordecai's people, the Jews, throughout the whole kingdom of Xerxes.

⁷In the twelfth year of King Xerxes, in the first month, the month of Nisan, the *pur* (that is, the lot) was cast in the presence of Haman to select a day and month. And the lot fell on[ʷ] the twelfth month, the month of Adar.

⁸Then Haman said to King Xerxes, "There is a certain people dispersed among the peoples in all the provinces of your kingdom who keep themselves separate. Their customs are different from those of all other people, and they do not obey the king's laws; it is not in the king's best interest to tolerate them. ⁹If it pleases the king, let a decree be issued to destroy them, and I will give ten thousand talents[ᵃ] of silver to the king's administrators for the royal treasury."

¹⁰So the king took his signet ring from his finger and gave it to Haman son of Hammedatha, the Agagite, the enemy of the Jews. ¹¹"Keep the money," the king said to Haman, "and do with the people as you please."

¹²Then on the thirteenth day of the first month the royal secretaries were summoned. They wrote out in the script of each province and in the

language of each people all Haman's orders to the king's satraps, the governors of the various provinces and the nobles of the various peoples. These were written in the name of King Xerxes himself and sealed with his own ring. ¹³Dispatches were sent by couriers to all the king's provinces with the order to destroy, kill and annihilate all the Jews—young and old, women and children—on a single day, the thirteenth day of the twelfth month, the month of Adar, and to plunder their goods. ¹⁴A copy of the text of the edict was to be issued as law in every province and made known to the people of every nationality so they would be ready for that day.

¹⁵The couriers went out, spurred on by the king's command, and the edict was issued in the citadel of Susa. The king and Haman sat down to drink, but the city of Susa was bewildered.

Esther 4 New International Version (NIV)

Mordecai Persuades Esther to Help

4 When Mordecai learned of all that had been done, he tore his clothes, put on sackcloth and ashes, and went out into the city, wailing loudly and bitterly. ²But he went only as far as the king's gate, because no one clothed in sackcloth was allowed to enter it. ³In every province to which the edict and order of the king came, there was great mourning among the Jews, with fasting, weeping and wailing. Many lay in sackcloth and ashes.

⁴When Esther's eunuchs and female attendants came and told her about Mordecai, she was in great distress. She sent clothes for him to put on instead of his sackcloth, but he would not accept them. ⁵Then Esther summoned Hathak, one of the king's eunuchs assigned to attend her, and ordered him to find out what was troubling Mordecai and why.

⁶So Hathak went out to Mordecai in the open square of the city in front of the king's gate. ⁷Mordecai told him everything that had happened to him, including the exact amount of money Haman had promised to pay into the royal treasury for the destruction of the Jews. ⁸He also gave him a copy of the text of the edict for their annihilation, which had been published in Susa,

to show to Esther and explain it to her, and he told him to instruct her to go into the king's presence to beg for mercy and plead with him for her people.

⁹Hathak went back and reported to Esther what Mordecai had said. ¹⁰Then she instructed him to say to Mordecai, ¹¹"All the king's officials and the people of the royal provinces know that for any man or woman who approaches the king in the inner court without being summoned the king has but one law: that they be put to death unless the king extends the gold scepter to them and spares their lives. But thirty days have passed since I was called to go to the king."

¹²When Esther's words were reported to Mordecai, ¹³he sent back this answer: "Do not think that because you are in the king's house you alone of all the Jews will escape. ¹⁴For if you remain silent at this time, relief and deliverance for the Jews will arise from another place, but you and your father's family will perish. And who knows but that you have come to your royal position for such a time as this?"

¹⁵Then Esther sent this reply to Mordecai: ¹⁶"Go, gather together all the Jews who are in Susa, and fast for me. Do not eat or drink for three days, night or day. I and my attendants will fast as you do. When this is done, I will go to the king, even though it is against the law. And if I perish, I perish."

¹⁷So Mordecai went away and carried out all of Esther's instructions.

Esther 5 New International Version (NIV)

Esther's Request to the King

5 On the third day Esther put on her royal robes and stood in the inner court of the palace, in front of the king's hall. The king was sitting on his royal throne in the hall, facing the entrance. ²When he saw Queen Esther standing in the court, he was pleased with her and held out to her the gold scepter that was in his hand. So Esther approached and touched the tip of the scepter.

³Then the king asked, "What is it, Queen Esther? What is your request? Even up to half the kingdom, it will be given you."

4"If it pleases the king," replied Esther, "let the king, together with Haman, come today to a banquet I have prepared for him."

5"Bring Haman at once," the king said, "so that we may do what Esther asks."

So the king and Haman went to the banquet Esther had prepared. 6As they were drinking wine, the king again asked Esther, "Now what is your petition? It will be given you. And what is your request? Even up to half the kingdom, it will be granted."

7Esther replied, "My petition and my request is this: 8If the king regards me with favor and if it pleases the king to grant my petition and fulfill my request, let the king and Haman come tomorrow to the banquet I will prepare for them. Then I will answer the king's question."

Haman's Rage Against Mordecai

9Haman went out that day happy and in high spirits. But when he saw Mordecai at the king's gate and observed that he neither rose nor showed fear in his presence, he was filled with rage against Mordecai. 10Nevertheless, Haman restrained himself and went home.

Calling together his friends and Zeresh, his wife, 11Haman boasted to them about his vast wealth, his many sons, and all the ways the king had honored him and how he had elevated him above the other nobles and officials. 12"And that's not all," Haman added. "I'm the only person Queen Esther invited to accompany the king to the banquet she gave. And she has invited me along with the king tomorrow. 13But all this gives me no satisfaction as long as I see that Jew Mordecai sitting at the king's gate."

14His wife Zeresh and all his friends said to him, "Have a pole set up, reaching to a height of fifty cubits,[a] and ask the king in the morning to have Mordecai impaled on it. Then go with the king to the banquet and enjoy yourself." This suggestion delighted Haman, and he had the pole set up.

Mordecai Honored

6 That night the king could not sleep; so he ordered the book of the chronicles, the record of his reign, to be brought in and read to him. ²It was found recorded there that Mordecai had exposed Bigthana and Teresh, two of the king's officers who guarded the doorway, who had conspired to assassinate King Xerxes.

³"What honor and recognition has Mordecai received for this?" the king asked.

"Nothing has been done for him," his attendants answered.

⁴The king said, "Who is in the court?" Now Haman had just entered the outer court of the palace to speak to the king about impaling Mordecai on the pole he had set up for him.

⁵His attendants answered, "Haman is standing in the court."

"Bring him in," the king ordered.

⁶When Haman entered, the king asked him, "What should be done for the man the king delights to honor?"

Now Haman thought to himself, "Who is there that the king would rather honor than me?" ⁷So he answered the king, "For the man the king delights to honor, ⁸have them bring a royal robe the king has worn and a horse the king has ridden, one with a royal crest placed on its head. ⁹Then let the robe and horse be entrusted to one of the king's most noble princes. Let them robe the man the king delights to honor, and lead him on the horse through the city streets, proclaiming before him, 'This is what is done for the man the king delights to honor!'"

¹⁰"Go at once," the king commanded Haman. "Get the robe and the horse and do just as you have suggested for Mordecai the Jew, who sits at the king's gate. Do not neglect anything you have recommended."

¹¹So Haman got the robe and the horse. He robed Mordecai, and led him on horseback through the city streets, proclaiming before him, "This is what is done for the man the king delights to honor!"

¹²Afterward Mordecai returned to the king's gate. But Haman rushed home, with his head covered in grief, ¹³and told Zeresh his wife and all his friends everything that had happened to him.

His advisers and his wife Zeresh said to him, "Since Mordecai, before whom your downfall has started, is of Jewish origin, you cannot stand against him—you will surely come to ruin!" ¹⁴While they were still talking with him, the king's eunuchs arrived and hurried Haman away to the banquet Esther had prepared.

Esther 7 New International Version (NIV)

Haman Impaled

7 So the king and Haman went to Queen Esther's banquet, ²and as they were drinking wine on the second day, the king again asked, "Queen Esther, what is your petition? It will be given you. What is your request? Even up to half the kingdom, it will be granted."

³Then Queen Esther answered, "If I have found favor with you, Your Majesty, and if it pleases you, grant me my life—this is my petition. And spare my people—this is my request. ⁴For I and my people have been sold to be destroyed, killed and annihilated. If we had merely been sold as male and female slaves, I would have kept quiet, because no such distress would justify disturbing the king.[a]"

⁵King Xerxes asked Queen Esther, "Who is he? Where is he—the man who has dared to do such a thing?"

⁶Esther said, "An adversary and enemy! This vile Haman!"

Then Haman was terrified before the king and queen. ⁷The king got up in a rage, left his wine and went out into the palace garden. But Haman, realizing that the king had already decided his fate, stayed behind to beg Queen Esther for his life.

⁸Just as the king returned from the palace garden to the banquet hall, Haman was falling on the couch where Esther was reclining.

The king exclaimed, "Will he even molest the queen while she is with me in the house?"

As soon as the word left the king's mouth, they covered Haman's face. ⁹Then Harbona, one of the eunuchs attending the king, said, "A pole reaching to a height of fifty cubits⁽ᵃ⁾ stands by Haman's house. He had it set up for Mordecai, who spoke up to help the king."

The king said, "Impale him on it!" ¹⁰So they impaled Haman on the pole he had set up for Mordecai. Then the king's fury subsided.

Esther 8 New International Version (NIV)

The King's Edict in Behalf of the Jews

8 That same day King Xerxes gave Queen Esther the estate of Haman, the enemy of the Jews. And Mordecai came into the presence of the king, for Esther had told how he was related to her. ²The king took off his signet ring, which he had reclaimed from Haman, and presented it to Mordecai. And Esther appointed him over Haman's estate.

³Esther again pleaded with the king, falling at his feet and weeping. She begged him to put an end to the evil plan of Haman the Agagite, which he had devised against the Jews. ⁴Then the king extended the gold scepter to Esther and she arose and stood before him.

⁵"If it pleases the king," she said, "and if he regards me with favor and thinks it the right thing to do, and if he is pleased with me, let an order be written overruling the dispatches that Haman son of Hammedatha, the Agagite, devised and wrote to destroy the Jews in all the king's provinces. ⁶For how can I bear to see disaster fall on my people? How can I bear to see the destruction of my family?"

[7] King Xerxes replied to Queen Esther and to Mordecai the Jew, "Because Haman attacked the Jews, I have given his estate to Esther, and they have impaled him on the pole he set up. [8] Now write another decree in the king's name in behalf of the Jews as seems best to you, and seal it with the king's signet ring—for no document written in the king's name and sealed with his ring can be revoked."

[9] At once the royal secretaries were summoned—on the twenty-third day of the third month, the month of Sivan. They wrote out all Mordecai's orders to the Jews, and to the satraps, governors and nobles of the 127 provinces stretching from India to Cush.[a] These orders were written in the script of each province and the language of each people and also to the Jews in their own script and language. [10] Mordecai wrote in the name of King Xerxes, sealed the dispatches with the king's signet ring, and sent them by mounted couriers, who rode fast horses especially bred for the king.

[11] The king's edict granted the Jews in every city the right to assemble and protect themselves; to destroy, kill and annihilate the armed men of any nationality or province who might attack them and their women and children,[a] and to plunder the property of their enemies. [12] The day appointed for the Jews to do this in all the provinces of King Xerxes was the thirteenth day of the twelfth month, the month of Adar. [13] A copy of the text of the edict was to be issued as law in every province and made known to the people of every nationality so that the Jews would be ready on that day to avenge themselves on their enemies.

[14] The couriers, riding the royal horses, went out, spurred on by the king's command, and the edict was issued in the citadel of Susa.

The Triumph of the Jews

[15] When Mordecai left the king's presence, he was wearing royal garments of blue and white, a large crown of gold and a purple robe of fine linen. And the city of Susa held a joyous celebration. [16] For the Jews it was a time of happiness and joy, gladness and honor. [17] In every province and in every city to which the edict of the king came, there was joy and gladness among the Jews, with feasting and celebrating. And many people of other nationalities became Jews because fear of the Jews had seized them.

104

9 On the thirteenth day of the twelfth month, the month of Adar, the edict commanded by the king was to be carried out. On this day the enemies of the Jews had hoped to overpower them, but now the tables were turned and the Jews got the upper hand over those who hated them. ²The Jews assembled in their cities in all the provinces of King Xerxes to attack those determined to destroy them. No one could stand against them, because the people of all the other nationalities were afraid of them. ³And all the nobles of the provinces, the satraps, the governors and the king's administrators helped the Jews, because fear of Mordecai had seized them. ⁴Mordecai was prominent in the palace; his reputation spread throughout the provinces, and he became more and more powerful.

⁵The Jews struck down all their enemies with the sword, killing and destroying them, and they did what they pleased to those who hated them. ⁶In the citadel of Susa, the Jews killed and destroyed five hundred men. ⁷They also killed Parshandatha, Dalphon, Aspatha, ⁸Poratha, Adalia, Aridatha, ⁹Parmashta, Arisai, Aridai and Vaizatha, ¹⁰the ten sons of Haman son of Hammedatha, the enemy of the Jews. But they did not lay their hands on the plunder.

¹¹The number of those killed in the citadel of Susa was reported to the king that same day. ¹²The king said to Queen Esther, "The Jews have killed and destroyed five hundred men and the ten sons of Haman in the citadel of Susa. What have they done in the rest of the king's provinces? Now what is your petition? It will be given you. What is your request? It will also be granted."

¹³"If it pleases the king," Esther answered, "give the Jews in Susa permission to carry out this day's edict tomorrow also, and let Haman's ten sons be impaled on poles."

¹⁴So the king commanded that this be done. An edict was issued in Susa, and they impaled the ten sons of Haman. ¹⁵The Jews in Susa came together on the fourteenth day of the month of Adar, and they put to death in Susa three hundred men, but they did not lay their hands on the plunder.

16 Meanwhile, the remainder of the Jews who were in the king's provinces also assembled to protect themselves and get relief from their enemies. They killed seventy-five thousand of them but did not lay their hands on the plunder. 17 This happened on the thirteenth day of the month of Adar, and on the fourteenth they rested and made it a day of feasting and joy.

18 The Jews in Susa, however, had assembled on the thirteenth and fourteenth, and then on the fifteenth they rested and made it a day of feasting and joy.

19 That is why rural Jews—those living in villages—observe the fourteenth of the month of Adar as a day of joy and feasting, a day for giving presents to each other.

Purim Established

20 Mordecai recorded these events, and he sent letters to all the Jews throughout the provinces of King Xerxes, near and far, 21 to have them celebrate annually the fourteenth and fifteenth days of the month of Adar 22 as the time when the Jews got relief from their enemies, and as the month when their sorrow was turned into joy and their mourning into a day of celebration. He wrote them to observe the days as days of feasting and joy and giving presents of food to one another and gifts to the poor.

23 So the Jews agreed to continue the celebration they had begun, doing what Mordecai had written to them. 24 For Haman son of Hammedatha, the Agagite, the enemy of all the Jews, had plotted against the Jews to destroy them and had cast the *pur* (that is, the lot) for their ruin and destruction. 25 But when the plot came to the king's attention,[a] he issued written orders that the evil scheme Haman had devised against the Jews should come back onto his own head, and that he and his sons should be impaled on poles. 26 (Therefore these days were called Purim, from the word *pur*.) Because of everything written in this letter and because of what they had seen and what had happened to them, 27 the Jews took it on themselves to establish the custom that they and their descendants and all who join them should without fail observe these two days every year, in the way prescribed and at the time appointed. 28 These days should be

remembered and observed in every generation by every family, and in every province and in every city. And these days of Purim should never fail to be celebrated by the Jews—nor should the memory of these days die out among their descendants.

²⁹So Queen Esther, daughter of Abihail, along with Mordecai the Jew, wrote with full authority to confirm this second letter concerning Purim. ³⁰And Mordecai sent letters to all the Jews in the 127 provinces of Xerxes' kingdom—words of goodwill and assurance— ³¹to establish these days of Purim at their designated times, as Mordecai the Jew and Queen Esther had decreed for them, and as they had established for themselves and their descendants in regard to their times of fasting and lamentation. ³²Esther's decree confirmed these regulations about Purim, and it was written down in the records.

Esther 10 New International Version (NIV)

The Greatness of Mordecai

10 King Xerxes imposed tribute throughout the empire, to its distant shores. ²And all his acts of power and might, together with a full account of the greatness of Mordecai, whom the king had promoted, are they not written in the book of the annals of the kings of Media and Persia? ³Mordecai the Jew was second in rank to King Xerxes, preeminent among the Jews, and held in high esteem by his many fellow Jews, because he worked for the good of his people and spoke up for the welfare of all the Jews.

Esther 1 King James Version (KJV)

1 Now it came to pass in the days of Ahasuerus, (this is Ahasuerus which reigned, from India even unto Ethiopia, over an hundred and seven and twenty provinces:)

2 That in those days, when the king Ahasuerus sat on the throne of his kingdom, which was in Shushan the palace,

3 In the third year of his reign, he made a feast unto all his princes and his servants; the power of Persia and Media, the nobles and princes of the provinces, being before him:

4 When he shewed the riches of his glorious kingdom and the honour of his excellent majesty many days, even an hundred and fourscore days.

5 And when these days were expired, the king made a feast unto all the people that were present in Shushan the palace, both unto great and small, seven days, in the court of the garden of the king's palace;

6 Where were white, green, and blue, hangings, fastened with cords of fine linen and purple to silver rings and pillars of marble: the beds were of gold and silver, upon a pavement of red, and blue, and white, and black, marble.

7 And they gave them drink in vessels of gold, (the vessels being diverse one from another,) and royal wine in abundance, according to the state of the king.

8 And the drinking was according to the law; none did compel: for so the king had appointed to all the officers of his house, that they should do according to every man's pleasure.

9 Also Vashti the queen made a feast for the women in the royal house which belonged to king Ahasuerus.

10 On the seventh day, when the heart of the king was merry with wine, he commanded Mehuman, Biztha, Harbona, Bigtha, and Abagtha, Zethar, and Carcas, the seven chamberlains that served in the presence of Ahasuerus the king,

11 To bring Vashti the queen before the king with the crown royal, to shew the people and the princes her beauty: for she was fair to look on.

¹²But the queen Vashti refused to come at the king's commandment by his chamberlains: therefore was the king very wroth, and his anger burned in him.

¹³Then the king said to the wise men, which knew the times, (for so was the king's manner toward all that knew law and judgment:

¹⁴And the next unto him was Carshena, Shethar, Admatha, Tarshish, Meres, Marsena, and Memucan, the seven princes of Persia and Media, which saw the king's face, and which sat the first in the kingdom;)

¹⁵What shall we do unto the queen Vashti according to law, because she hath not performed the commandment of the king Ahasuerus by the chamberlains?

¹⁶And Memucan answered before the king and the princes, Vashti the queen hath not done wrong to the king only, but also to all the princes, and to all the people that are in all the provinces of the king Ahasuerus.

¹⁷For this deed of the queen shall come abroad unto all women, so that they shall despise their husbands in their eyes, when it shall be reported, The king Ahasuerus commanded Vashti the queen to be brought in before him, but she came not.

¹⁸Likewise shall the ladies of Persia and Media say this day unto all the king's princes, which have heard of the deed of the queen. Thus shall there arise too much contempt and wrath.

¹⁹If it please the king, let there go a royal commandment from him, and let it be written among the laws of the Persians and the Medes, that it be not altered, That Vashti come no more before king Ahasuerus; and let the king give her royal estate unto another that is better than she.

²⁰And when the king's decree which he shall make shall be published throughout all his empire, (for it is great,) all the wives shall give to their husbands honour, both to great and small.

²¹And the saying pleased the king and the princes; and the king did according to the word of Memucan:

²²For he sent letters into all the king's provinces, into every province according to the writing thereof, and to every people after their language, that every man should bear rule in his own house, and that it should be published according to the language of every people.

Esther 2 King James Version (KJV)
2 After these things, when the wrath of king Ahasuerus was appeased, he remembered Vashti, and what she had done, and what was decreed against her.

²Then said the king's servants that ministered unto him, Let there be fair young virgins sought for the king:

³And let the king appoint officers in all the provinces of his kingdom, that they may gather together all the fair young virgins unto Shushan the palace, to the house of the women, unto the custody of Hege the king's chamberlain, keeper of the women; and let their things for purification be given them:

⁴And let the maiden which pleaseth the king be queen instead of Vashti. And the thing pleased the king; and he did so.

⁵Now in Shushan the palace there was a certain Jew, whose name was Mordecai, the son of Jair, the son of Shimei, the son of Kish, a Benjamite;

⁶Who had been carried away from Jerusalem with the captivity which had been carried away with Jeconiah king of Judah, whom Nebuchadnezzar the king of Babylon had carried away.

⁷And he brought up Hadassah, that is, Esther, his uncle's daughter: for she had neither father nor mother, and the maid was fair and beautiful; whom Mordecai, when her father and mother were dead, took for his own daughter.

⁸So it came to pass, when the king's commandment and his decree was heard, and when many maidens were gathered together unto Shushan the palace, to the custody of Hegai, that Esther was brought also unto the king's house, to the custody of Hegai, keeper of the women.

110

⁹And the maiden pleased him, and she obtained kindness of him; and he speedily gave her her things for purification, with such things as belonged to her, and seven maidens, which were meet to be given her, out of the king's house: and he preferred her and her maids unto the best place of the house of the women.

¹⁰Esther had not shewed her people nor her kindred: for Mordecai had charged her that she should not shew it.

¹¹And Mordecai walked every day before the court of the women's house, to know how Esther did, and what should become of her.

¹²Now when every maid's turn was come to go in to king Ahasuerus, after that she had been twelve months, according to the manner of the women, (for so were the days of their purifications accomplished, to wit, six months with oil of myrrh, and six months with sweet odours, and with other things for the purifying of the women;)

¹³Then thus came every maiden unto the king; whatsoever she desired was given her to go with her out of the house of the women unto the king's house.

¹⁴In the evening she went, and on the morrow she returned into the second house of the women, to the custody of Shaashgaz, the king's chamberlain, which kept the concubines: she came in unto the king no more, except the king delighted in her, and that she were called by name.

¹⁵Now when the turn of Esther, the daughter of Abihail the uncle of Mordecai, who had taken her for his daughter, was come to go in unto the king, she required nothing but what Hegai the king's chamberlain, the keeper of the women, appointed. And Esther obtained favour in the sight of all them that looked upon her.

¹⁶So Esther was taken unto king Ahasuerus into his house royal in the tenth month, which is the month Tebeth, in the seventh year of his reign.

¹⁷And the king loved Esther above all the women, and she obtained grace and favour in his sight more than all the virgins; so that he set the royal crown upon her head, and made her queen instead of Vashti.

¹⁸ Then the king made a great feast unto all his princes and his servants, even Esther's feast; and he made a release to the provinces, and gave gifts, according to the state of the king.

¹⁹ And when the virgins were gathered together the second time, then Mordecai sat in the king's gate.

²⁰ Esther had not yet shewed her kindred nor her people; as Mordecai had charged her: for Esther did the commandment of Mordecai, like as when she was brought up with him.

²¹ In those days, while Mordecai sat in the king's gate, two of the king's chamberlains, Bigthan and Teresh, of those which kept the door, were wroth, and sought to lay hands on the king Ahasuerus.

²² And the thing was known to Mordecai, who told it unto Esther the queen; and Esther certified the king thereof in Mordecai's name.

²³ And when inquisition was made of the matter, it was found out; therefore they were both hanged on a tree: and it was written in the book of the chronicles before the king.

Esther 3 King James Version (KJV)

3 After these things did king Ahasuerus promote Haman the son of Hammedatha the Agagite, and advanced him, and set his seat above all the princes that were with him.

² And all the king's servants, that were in the king's gate, bowed, and reverenced Haman: for the king had so commanded concerning him. But Mordecai bowed not, nor did him reverence.

³ Then the king's servants, which were in the king's gate, said unto Mordecai, Why transgressest thou the king's commandment?

⁴ Now it came to pass, when they spake daily unto him, and he hearkened not unto them, that they told Haman, to see whether Mordecai's matters would stand: for he had told them that he was a Jew.

⁵ And when Haman saw that Mordecai bowed not, nor did him reverence, then was Haman full of wrath.

⁶And he thought scorn to lay hands on Mordecai alone; for they had shewed him the people of Mordecai: wherefore Haman sought to destroy all the Jews that were throughout the whole kingdom of Ahasuerus, even the people of Mordecai.

⁷In the first month, that is, the month Nisan, in the twelfth year of king Ahasuerus, they cast Pur, that is, the lot, before Haman from day to day, and from month to month, to the twelfth month, that is, the month Adar.

⁸And Haman said unto king Ahasuerus, There is a certain people scattered abroad and dispersed among the people in all the provinces of thy kingdom; and their laws are diverse from all people; neither keep they the king's laws: therefore it is not for the king's profit to suffer them.

⁹If it please the king, let it be written that they may be destroyed: and I will pay ten thousand talents of silver to the hands of those that have the charge of the business, to bring it into the king's treasuries.

¹⁰And the king took his ring from his hand, and gave it unto Haman the son of Hammedatha the Agagite, the Jews' enemy.

¹¹And the king said unto Haman, The silver is given to thee, the people also, to do with them as it seemeth good to thee.

¹²Then were the king's scribes called on the thirteenth day of the first month, and there was written according to all that Haman had commanded unto the king's lieutenants, and to the governors that were over every province, and to the rulers of every people of every province according to the writing thereof, and to every people after their language; in the name of king Ahasuerus was it written, and sealed with the king's ring.

¹³And the letters were sent by posts into all the king's provinces, to destroy, to kill, and to cause to perish, all Jews, both young and old, little children and women, in one day, even upon the thirteenth day of the twelfth month, which is the month Adar, and to take the spoil of them for a prey.

¹⁴The copy of the writing for a commandment to be given in every province was published unto all people, that they should be ready against that day.

¹⁴The posts went out, being hastened by the king's commandment, and the decree was given in Shushan the palace. And the king and Haman sat down to drink; but the city Shushan was perplexed.

Esther 4 King James Version (KJV)

4 When Mordecai perceived all that was done, Mordecai rent his clothes, and put on sackcloth with ashes, and went out into the midst of the city, and cried with a loud and a bitter cry;

²And came even before the king's gate: for none might enter into the king's gate clothed with sackcloth.

³And in every province, whithersoever the king's commandment and his decree came, there was great mourning among the Jews, and fasting, and weeping, and wailing; and many lay in sackcloth and ashes.

⁴So Esther's maids and her chamberlains came and told it her. Then was the queen exceedingly grieved; and she sent raiment to clothe Mordecai, and to take away his sackcloth from him: but he received it not.

⁵Then called Esther for Hatach, one of the king's chamberlains, whom he had appointed to attend upon her, and gave him a commandment to Mordecai, to know what it was, and why it was.

⁶So Hatach went forth to Mordecai unto the street of the city, which was before the king's gate.

⁷And Mordecai told him of all that had happened unto him, and of the sum of the money that Haman had promised to pay to the king's treasuries for the Jews, to destroy them.

⁸Also he gave him the copy of the writing of the decree that was given at Shushan to destroy them, to shew it unto Esther, and to declare it unto her, and to charge her that she should go in unto the king, to make supplication unto him, and to make request before him for her people.

⁹And Hatach came and told Esther the words of Mordecai.

¹⁰Again Esther spake unto Hatach, and gave him commandment unto Mordecai;

11 All the king's servants, and the people of the king's provinces, do know, that whosoever, whether man or women, shall come unto the king into the inner court, who is not called, there is one law of his to put him to death, except such to whom the king shall hold out the golden sceptre, that he may live: but I have not been called to come in unto the king these thirty days.

12 And they told to Mordecai Esther's words.

13 Then Mordecai commanded to answer Esther, Think not with thyself that thou shalt escape in the king's house, more than all the Jews.

14 For if thou altogether holdest thy peace at this time, then shall there enlargement and deliverance arise to the Jews from another place; but thou and thy father's house shall be destroyed: and who knoweth whether thou art come to the kingdom for such a time as this?

15 Then Esther bade them return Mordecai this answer,

16 Go, gather together all the Jews that are present in Shushan, and fast ye for me, and neither eat nor drink three days, night or day: I also and my maidens will fast likewise; and so will I go in unto the king, which is not according to the law: and if I perish, I perish.

17 So Mordecai went his way, and did according to all that Esther had commanded him.

Esther 5 King James Version (KJV)

5 Now it came to pass on the third day, that Esther put on her royal apparel, and stood in the inner court of the king's house, over against the king's house: and the king sat upon his royal throne in the royal house, over against the gate of the house.

²And it was so, when the king saw Esther the queen standing in the court, that she obtained favour in his sight: and the king held out to Esther the golden sceptre that was in his hand. So Esther drew near, and touched the top of the sceptre.

³Then said the king unto her, What wilt thou, queen Esther? and what is thy request? it shall be even given thee to the half of the kingdom.

⁴And Esther answered, If it seem good unto the king, let the king and Haman come this day unto the banquet that I have prepared for him.

⁵Then the king said, Cause Haman to make haste, that he may do as Esther hath said. So the king and Haman came to the banquet that Esther had prepared.

⁶And the king said unto Esther at the banquet of wine, What is thy petition? and it shall be granted thee: and what is thy request? even to the half of the kingdom it shall be performed.

⁷Then answered Esther, and said, My petition and my request is;

⁸If I have found favour in the sight of the king, and if it please the king to grant my petition, and to perform my request, let the king and Haman come to the banquet that I shall prepare for them, and I will do to morrow as the king hath said.

⁹Then went Haman forth that day joyful and with a glad heart: but when Haman saw Mordecai in the king's gate, that he stood not up, nor moved for him, he was full of indignation against Mordecai.

¹⁰Nevertheless Haman refrained himself: and when he came home, he sent and called for his friends, and Zeresh his wife.

¹¹And Haman told them of the glory of his riches, and the multitude of his children, and all the things wherein the king had promoted him, and how he had advanced him above the princes and servants of the king.

¹²Haman said moreover, Yea, Esther the queen did let no man come in with the king unto the banquet that she had prepared but myself; and to morrow am I invited unto her also with the king.

¹³Yet all this availeth me nothing, so long as I see Mordecai the Jew sitting at the king's gate.

¹⁴Then said Zeresh his wife and all his friends unto him, Let a gallows be made of fifty cubits high, and to morrow speak thou unto the king that Mordecai may be hanged thereon: then go thou in merrily with the king unto the banquet. And the thing pleased Haman; and he caused the gallows to be made.

Esther 6 King James Version (KJV)

6 On that night could not the king sleep, and he commanded to bring the book of records of the chronicles; and they were read before the king.

²And it was found written, that Mordecai had told of Bigthana and Teresh, two of the king's chamberlains, the keepers of the door, who sought to lay hand on the king Ahasuerus.

³And the king said, What honour and dignity hath been done to Mordecai for this? Then said the king's servants that ministered unto him, There is nothing done for him.

⁴And the king said, Who is in the court? Now Haman was come into the outward court of the king's house, to speak unto the king to hang Mordecai on the gallows that he had prepared for him.

⁵And the king's servants said unto him, Behold, Haman standeth in the court. And the king said, Let him come in.

⁶So Haman came in. And the king said unto him, What shall be done unto the man whom the king delighteth to honour? Now Haman thought in his heart, To whom would the king delight to do honour more than to myself?

⁷And Haman answered the king, For the man whom the king delighteth to honour,

⁸Let the royal apparel be brought which the king useth to wear, and the horse that the king rideth upon, and the crown royal which is set upon his head:

⁹And let this apparel and horse be delivered to the hand of one of the king's most noble princes, that they may array the man withal whom the king delighteth to honour, and bring him on horseback through the street of the city, and proclaim before him, Thus shall it be done to the man whom the king delighteth to honour.

¹⁰Then the king said to Haman, Make haste, and take the apparel and the horse, as thou hast said, and do even so to Mordecai the Jew, that sitteth at the king's gate: let nothing fail of all that thou hast spoken.

¹¹Then took Haman the apparel and the horse, and arrayed Mordecai, and brought him on horseback through the street of the city, and proclaimed before him, Thus shall it be done unto the man whom the king delighteth to honour.

¹²And Mordecai came again to the king's gate. But Haman hasted to his house mourning, and having his head covered.

¹³And Haman told Zeresh his wife and all his friends every thing that had befallen him. Then said his wise men and Zeresh his wife unto him, If Mordecai be of the seed of the Jews, before whom thou hast begun to fall, thou shalt not prevail against him, but shalt surely fall before him.

¹⁴And while they were yet talking with him, came the king's chamberlains, and hasted to bring Haman unto the banquet that Esther had prepared.

Esther 7 King James Version (KJV)

7 So the king and Haman came to banquet with Esther the queen.

2And the king said again unto Esther on the second day at the banquet of wine, What is thy petition, queen Esther? and it shall be granted thee: and what is thy request? and it shall be performed, even to the half of the kingdom.

3Then Esther the queen answered and said, If I have found favour in thy sight, O king, and if it please the king, let my life be given me at my petition, and my people at my request:

4For we are sold, I and my people, to be destroyed, to be slain, and to perish. But if we had been sold for bondmen and bondwomen, I had held my tongue, although the enemy could not countervail the king's damage.

5Then the king Ahasuerus answered and said unto Esther the queen, Who is he, and where is he, that durst presume in his heart to do so?

6And Esther said, The adversary and enemy is this wicked Haman. Then Haman was afraid before the king and the queen.

7And the king arising from the banquet of wine in his wrath went into the palace garden: and Haman stood up to make request for his life to Esther the queen; for he saw that there was evil determined against him by the king.

8Then the king returned out of the palace garden into the place of the banquet of wine; and Haman was fallen upon the bed whereon Esther was. Then said the king, Will he force the queen also before me in the house? As the word went out of king's mouth, they covered Haman's face.

9And Harbonah, one of the chamberlains, said before the king, Behold also, the gallows fifty cubits high, which Haman had made for Mordecai, who spoken good for the king, standeth in the house of Haman. Then the king said, Hang him thereon.

10So they hanged Haman on the gallows that he had prepared for Mordecai. Then was the king's wrath pacified.

8 On that day did the king Ahasuerus give the house of Haman the Jews' enemy unto Esther the queen. And Mordecai came before the king; for Esther had told what he was unto her.

²And the king took off his ring, which he had taken from Haman, and gave it unto Mordecai. And Esther set Mordecai over the house of Haman.

³And Esther spake yet again before the king, and fell down at his feet, and besought him with tears to put away the mischief of Haman the Agagite, and his device that he had devised against the Jews.

⁴Then the king held out the golden sceptre toward Esther. So Esther arose, and stood before the king,

⁵And said, If it please the king, and if I have favour in his sight, and the thing seem right before the king, and I be pleasing in his eyes, let it be written to reverse the letters devised by Haman the son of Hammedatha the Agagite, which he wrote to destroy the Jews which are in all the king's provinces:

⁶For how can I endure to see the evil that shall come unto my people? or how can I endure to see the destruction of my kindred?

⁷Then the king Ahasuerus said unto Esther the queen and to Mordecai the Jew, Behold, I have given Esther the house of Haman, and him they have hanged upon the gallows, because he laid his hand upon the Jews.

⁸Write ye also for the Jews, as it liketh you, in the king's name, and seal it with the king's ring: for the writing which is written in the king's name, and sealed with the king's ring, may no man reverse.

⁹Then were the king's scribes called at that time in the third month, that is, the month Sivan, on the three and twentieth day thereof; and it was written according to all that Mordecai commanded unto the Jews, and to the lieutenants, and the deputies and rulers of the provinces which are from India unto Ethiopia, an hundred twenty and seven provinces, unto every province according to the writing thereof, and unto every people after their language, and to the Jews according to their writing, and according to their language.

[10]And he wrote in the king Ahasuerus' name, and sealed it with the king's ring, and sent letters by posts on horseback, and riders on mules, camels, and young dromedaries:

[11]Wherein the king granted the Jews which were in every city to gather themselves together, and to stand for their life, to destroy, to slay and to cause to perish, all the power of the people and province that would assault them, both little ones and women, and to take the spoil of them for a prey,

[12]Upon one day in all the provinces of king Ahasuerus, namely, upon the thirteenth day of the twelfth month, which is the month Adar.

[13]The copy of the writing for a commandment to be given in every province was published unto all people, and that the Jews should be ready against that day to avenge themselves on their enemies.

[14]So the posts that rode upon mules and camels went out, being hastened and pressed on by the king's commandment. And the decree was given at Shushan the palace.

[15]And Mordecai went out from the presence of the king in royal apparel of blue and white, and with a great crown of gold, and with a garment of fine linen and purple: and the city of Shushan rejoiced and was glad.

[16]The Jews had light, and gladness, and joy, and honour.

[17]And in every province, and in every city, whithersoever the king's commandment and his decree came, the Jews had joy and gladness, a feast and a good day. And many of the people of the land became Jews; for the fear of the Jews fell upon them.

Esther 9 King James Version (KJV)

9 Now in the twelfth month, that is, the month Adar, on the thirteenth day of the same, when the king's commandment and his decree drew near to be put in execution, in the day that the enemies of the Jews hoped to have power over them, (though it was turned to the contrary, that the Jews had rule over them that hated them;)

2 The Jews gathered themselves together in their cities throughout all the provinces of the king Ahasuerus, to lay hand on such as sought their hurt: and no man could withstand them; for the fear of them fell upon all people.

3 And all the rulers of the provinces, and the lieutenants, and the deputies, and officers of the king, helped the Jews; because the fear of Mordecai fell upon them.

4 For Mordecai was great in the king's house, and his fame went out throughout all the provinces: for this man Mordecai waxed greater and greater.

5 Thus the Jews smote all their enemies with the stroke of the sword, and slaughter, and destruction, and did what they would unto those that hated them.

6 And in Shushan the palace the Jews slew and destroyed five hundred men.

7 And Parshandatha, and Dalphon, and Aspatha,

8 And Poratha, and Adalia, and Aridatha,

9 And Parmashta, and Arisai, and Aridai, and Vajezatha,

10 The ten sons of Haman the son of Hammedatha, the enemy of the Jews, slew they; but on the spoil laid they not their hand.

11 On that day the number of those that were slain in Shushan the palace was brought before the king.

12 And the king said unto Esther the queen, The Jews have slain and destroyed five hundred men in Shushan the palace, and the ten sons of Haman; what have they done in the rest of the king's provinces? now what is thy petition? and it shall be granted thee: or what is thy request further? and it shall be done.

¹³Then said Esther, If it please the king, let it be granted to the Jews which are in Shushan to do to morrow also according unto this day's decree, and let Haman's ten sons be hanged upon the gallows.

¹⁴And the king commanded it so to be done: and the decree was given at Shushan; and they hanged Haman's ten sons.

¹⁵For the Jews that were in Shushan gathered themselves together on the fourteenth day also of the month Adar, and slew three hundred men at Shushan; but on the prey they laid not their hand.

¹⁶But the other Jews that were in the king's provinces gathered themselves together, and stood for their lives, and had rest from their enemies, and slew of their foes seventy and five thousand, but they laid not their hands on the prey,

¹⁷On the thirteenth day of the month Adar; and on the fourteenth day of the same rested they, and made it a day of feasting and gladness.

¹⁸But the Jews that were at Shushan assembled together on the thirteenth day thereof, and on the fourteenth thereof; and on the fifteenth day of the same they rested, and made it a day of feasting and gladness.

¹⁹Therefore the Jews of the villages, that dwelt in the unwalled towns, made the fourteenth day of the month Adar a day of gladness and feasting, and a good day, and of sending portions one to another.

²⁰And Mordecai wrote these things, and sent letters unto all the Jews that were in all the provinces of the king Ahasuerus, both nigh and far,

²¹To stablish this among them, that they should keep the fourteenth day of the month Adar, and the fifteenth day of the same, yearly,

²²As the days wherein the Jews rested from their enemies, and the month which was turned unto them from sorrow to joy, and from mourning into a good day: that they should make them days of feasting and joy, and of sending portions one to another, and gifts to the poor.

²³And the Jews undertook to do as they had begun, and as Mordecai had written unto them;

²⁴Because Haman the son of Hammedatha, the Agagite, the enemy of all the Jews, had devised against the Jews to destroy them, and had cast Pur, that is, the lot, to consume them, and to destroy them;

²⁵But when Esther came before the king, he commanded by letters that his wicked device, which he devised against the Jews, should return upon his own head, and that he and his sons should be hanged on the gallows.

²⁶Wherefore they called these days Purim after the name of Pur. Therefore for all the words of this letter, and of that which they had seen concerning this matter, and which had come unto them,

²⁷The Jews ordained, and took upon them, and upon their seed, and upon all such as joined themselves unto them, so as it should not fail, that they would keep these two days according to their writing, and according to their appointed time every year;

²⁸And that these days should be remembered and kept throughout every generation, every family, every province, and every city; and that these days of Purim should not fail from among the Jews, nor the memorial of them perish from their seed.

²⁹Then Esther the queen, the daughter of Abihail, and Mordecai the Jew, wrote with all authority, to confirm this second letter of Purim.

³⁰And he sent the letters unto all the Jews, to the hundred twenty and seven provinces of the kingdom of Ahasuerus, with words of peace and truth,

³¹To confirm these days of Purim in their times appointed, according as Mordecai the Jew and Esther the queen had enjoined them, and as they had decreed for themselves and for their seed, the matters of the fastings and their cry.

³²And the decree of Esther confirmed these matters of Purim; and it was written in the book.

Esther 10 King James Version (KJV)

10 And the king Ahasuerus laid a tribute upon the land, and upon the isles of the sea.

²And all the acts of his power and of his might, and the declaration of the greatness of Mordecai, whereunto the king advanced him, are they not written in the book of the chronicles of the kings of Media and Persia?

³For Mordecai the Jew was next unto king Ahasuerus, and great among the Jews, and accepted of the multitude of his brethren, seeking the wealth of his people, and speaking peace to all his seed.

ESTHER - *Wife*

QUESTION	ANSWER
What does the name Esther mean?	Star
Who reared Esther?	Mordecai
In what country did the story of Esther take place?	In Persia
In what city did the main part of the story of Esther take place?	Susa or Shusban in Persia.
About what year did the main part of the story take place?	About 474 B.C.
How did the Jews come to be in Persia?	They were the descendants of the Jews who were carried away as captives by Nebuchadnezzar in 586 B.C.
In what country was Esther born?	Persia.
What was Esther's original name?	Hadassah
Where is the Book of Esther to be found in the Bible?	In the Old Testament, between Nehemiah and Job.
What is peculiar about the Book of Esther?	The word "GOD" does not appear in this book.
Who was Ahasuerus' queen before Esther?	Vashti
Why was the first queen divorced and banished from the palace?	She refused to appear before the king's drunken court at an improper time, and the king felt that the refusal was setting a bad example for the women of the kingdom.
By what other name is the Biblical Ahasuerus known?	Xerxes
What was Mordecai's relation to Esther?	Cousin
What position did Mordecai hold?	Hebrew minister at the court of Persia.
Who was Haman?	Prime Minister to the King.
Who caused the edict to go forth that all Jews were to be killed?	Haman
What happened to Haman?	He was hanged on the same gallows he had built for Mordecai.
What does the name Hadassah mean?	The Myrtle.
With other great Biblical character can Esther be compared?	King Solomon.
Who said: "And who knoweth whether thou art come to the kingdom for such a time as this"?	Mordecai to Esther.
How long was the preparation period for maidens who were to go before the king?	Twelve Months.

126

When was Esther made queen?	During the seventh year of the reign of Ahasuerus.
What made Haman so angry with Mordecai?	Mordecai would not bow before him or give him reverence.
What did Mordecai do when he learned of the edict to destroy the Jews?	He tore his clothes and put on sackcloth and ashes, and cried bitterly in the midst of the city.
Who pleaded with Esther to go before the king and try to save her people?	Mordecai
How many feasts did Esther prepare for the king in order to save her people?	Two
How long did Esther fast before going to the king?	Three days.
What present day feast commemorates Esther's Victory for her people?	The Feast of Purim or the Feast of Lots.
What is the significance of the sign of this degree?	It is an appeal to intelligence and emotion guided by God.
The color of the degree is symbolic of what?	Innocence and purity.
What is the flower of this degree?	The Lily of the field.
What does the flower of this degree stand for?	Peace and Purity.
What does the flower teach?	To keep ourselves unspotted from the world.
What further lesson may be learned from this flower?	True followers of Christ have been washed white by the Blood of the Lamb.
What attribute does this degree teach us to cultivate?	Courage.
What jewel is dedicated to Esther?	The Diamond (White)
What heavenly body is a symbol of this degree?	The Sun.
The dual symbols of the Crown and Scepter signify what?	Royalty and power.
What do the Crown and Scepter remind us of?	True friendship refuses no pain or loss for the object of its love.
What is the Star point emblem of this degree?	Crown and Scepter
What word belongs to this degree?	PURE
How many chapters are there in the Book of Esther?	Ten
Why is the sun an appropriate emblem for Esther?	Because Esther was a light and a power to her people.
What is the Christ symbol for this degree?	The Sun (The Sun of Righteousness)

What other designation doe the degree have?	The wife's degree.
What great lesson does this degree teach?	The willingness to sacrifice for a good cause, and faithfulness to kindred and friends.

Esther

Esther is the third Star Point Heroine

REPRESENTS

Esther represents the Ideal Wife because she not only succeeded in filling her duty to her husband but also maintained her high standards and performed her duty to God and her nation. As a result of Esther's influence and example, Ahasuerus used his power and authority to save the whole Jewish race from extinction.

THE MEANING OF THE NAME

Esther is the second name that was given to the daughter of Abihail. Esther means "Star" in Persian. Her first name was Hadassah which means "myrtle" in the ancient language of Chaldee. The name Esther was appropriate for this outstanding biblical personality. Her intercession on behalf of her people was like a star of hope and encouragement to a people enslaved, subjugated, and distant from her native land.

COLOR

The white billowy clouds and drifting snow is the color dedicated to Esther. It is appropriate to this Star Point because Esther, is feted, crowned, beautiful and wealthy, succeeded in remaining pure, upright and simple. Her life and actions were free from blemish and in every way, Esther was above reproach.

FLOWER

The chaste pure white lily, which has been recognized for generations is the symbol of purity and peace. Esther's effort to maintain purity of purpose and her effort to re-establish peaceful conditions between the conquered and the conqueror have made the dedication of the lily to her appropriate.

IDEALS

The ideals of the Third Star Point are pure and self-sacrifice. We may emulate these attributes by remaining faithful to our high standards and by conducting ourselves in every situation in such a notion that we may remain above reproach.

EMBLEMS

The Crown and Sceptre, used together, is the emblem for Esther. It symbolizes the force of power and authority used to achieve justice for all.

SYMBOL

The Sun is symbolic of the deeper meaning of the story of Esther. The sun, the source of light, power and strength symbolizes the enlightened leadership of Esther which made her the strength and power of the Jewish people. Christ the Sun of Righteousness, was and is the Enlightenment of the world and was and is a source of power and strength of all men.

JEWEL

The flawless, durable, and valuable diamond is dedicated to the office of Esther. Her character was flawless, her standards and beliefs durable, and her life as she lived it, was great value to her people.

BEATITUDE

The seventh Beatitude is associated with Esther. "Blessed are the peacemakers for they shall be called the children of God."

THE STORY

The Book of Esther

Vashti, the wife of Ahaseurus had been vanished from her position in the palace. A group of young girls, which was actually a harem was established according to definite customs. These young girls were chosen purely bon the basis of their natural beauty and purity. Mordecai, a cousin of Esther had brought the lovely Esther to the palace as one of the candidates for the queen ship.

Read the Book of Esther

Story of Martha

Martha

Definition	Fortitude and Abiding Faith
Degree	Sister
Gem	Emerald
Flower	Evergreen/Fern
Teaching	Hopeful
Emblem	Broken Column
Color	Green (Hope & Immortality)
Beatitude	2nd Beatitude (Matthew 5:4)
Verse Reference	John 11:1-26
Song	What a Friend We Have in Jesus
Season	Winter
Pass	Believest thou this

MARTHA

4th POINT OF THE STAR

Degree	Sister
Meaning	Instructed by Christ Abiding
Color	Green
Flower	Fern or Evergreen
Emblem	Broken Column
Symbol	Lamb & Cross

PASS
Believes thou this?
(Spoken by Jesus)

BEATITUDE
Blessed are them that mourn, for they shall be comforted.

JEWEL
Emerald

SEASON
Winter

133

MARTHA

The Sister

Bethany is a small village situated on the southeast side of the Mount of Olives, less than two miles from Jerusalem on the road from Jericho to Jerusalem No mention is made of this village :in the canonical books or in the Apocrypha of the Old Testament. Bethany makes it appearance for the first time, as does the Fourth Star Point in the New Testament. The more recent writers of biblical history speak of it as a miserable, untidy and tumble-down village. Actual or impending decay would seem be written upon its dwellings. Yet, we are filled with reverential awe as we recall the immortal memories of what occurred within and around this little village.

There is very little authentic information about the early history of Martha, Mary and Lazarus. It would seem that they were an orphan family. Their home is said to have been a very beautiful and wealthy home, with even luxuries. Martha was the housekeeper. She looked after the food, comforts of the family, and the guests. The central figure of the whole story, however, is Jesus, with Martha and Mary standing: in the foreground of the life of Jesus. Time and time again we find the Master, amidst the tumults, storm, applause's and successes of public life, taking refuge in some secluded or quiet spot, literally yearning for the privacy and the atmosphere of domestic life and home love. It is not known when Jesus began to make their home, his home when in Bethany. Christ on leaving his earthly father's home in Nazareth became a wanderer. He never had a home of his own on earth. One of the most striking and pathetic utterances He ever made regarding himself was in reference to his having no home, "the foxes have holes, and the birds of the air have nests; but the Son of Man hath not where to lay his head.11 His loneliness is manifest by his frequent communion with the Father.

The home at Bethany was to Him a home of quiet and rest, where a most cordial and loving welcome was extended with sincere affection. What a beautiful friendship sprang up between Jesus and every member of the Bethany family! The home was one of friendly peace that was not tainted with interested ambition. Martha is the patron saint of all good housewives, careful mothers, and skillful and efficient nurses of the present generation. Her character makes a strong appeal to energetic women and especially to comfort- loving men.

Dr. Rob Morris in The Rosary of the Eastern Star, written in 1865, sets forth the Christian application of the fourth point of the emblematic star in the following words:

"The tender and affectionate Martha, equally devoted to her Divine Friend, whether as the grateful guest of the life-giving God, whether she was "Cumbered with such serving" for his entertainment, or kneeling before him in the abandonment of sorrow or

134

walking with him weeping, to the sepulcher of her brother, is best represented under the guise of the meek and uncomplaining Lamb. "God has provided" her "a Lamb" for our delighted study. She is a Lamb "without blemish" in her display of womanly, social and Christian virtues, and she is one those who are described in the latter books of Divine law as being "made white in the blood of the Lamb," and "written in the Lamb's book of life."

Color: The color appropriate to the degree is GREEN, emblematical of the immutable nature of Truth and its victory.

Badge: Sister Martha, the badge of your office is the Broken Column within the Triangle, symbolic of life's uncertainty, and reminding you of the comfort which Martha received from her unswerving faith in God in the time of her sorrow. The Broken Column is an expressive emblem of the uncertainty of human existence, and the outward evidence of the decease of a young man cut down in the vigor of life.

Sign of the Sister: Join the hands together at the tips of the thumbs and fingers, forming the figure of a triangle.

Raise the triangle thus formed directly above the eyes.

Raise the eyes, looking through the triangle.

Pass: "Believest thou this!" A member on seeing this Sister's sign should respond with these words.

John 11 King James Version (KJV)

11 Now a certain man was sick, named Lazarus, of Bethany, the town of Mary and her sister Martha.

²(It was that Mary which anointed the Lord with ointment, and wiped his feet with her hair, whose brother Lazarus was sick.)

³Therefore his sisters sent unto him, saying, Lord, behold, he whom thou lovest is sick.

⁴When Jesus heard that, he said, This sickness is not unto death, but for the glory of God, that the Son of God might be glorified thereby.

⁵Now Jesus loved Martha, and her sister, and Lazarus.

⁶When he had heard therefore that he was sick, he abode two days still in the same place where he was.

⁷Then after that saith he to his disciples, Let us go into Judaea again.

⁸His disciples say unto him, Master, the Jews of late sought to stone thee; and goest thou thither again?

⁹Jesus answered, Are there not twelve hours in the day? If any man walk in the day, he stumbleth not, because he seeth the light of this world.

¹⁰But if a man walk in the night, he stumbleth, because there is no light in him.

¹¹These things said he: and after that he saith unto them, Our friend Lazarus sleepeth; but I go, that I may awake him out of sleep.

¹²Then said his disciples, Lord, if he sleep, he shall do well.

¹³Howbeit Jesus spake of his death: but they thought that he had spoken of taking of rest in sleep.

¹⁴Then said Jesus unto them plainly, Lazarus is dead.

¹⁵And I am glad for your sakes that I was not there, to the intent ye may believe; nevertheless let us go unto him.

¹⁶Then said Thomas, which is called Didymus, unto his fellow disciples, Let us also go, that we may die with him.

¹⁷Then when Jesus came, he found that he had lain in the grave four days already.

¹⁸Now Bethany was nigh unto Jerusalem, about fifteen furlongs off:

¹⁹And many of the Jews came to Martha and Mary, to comfort them concerning their brother.

²⁰Then Martha, as soon as she heard that Jesus was coming, went and met him: but Mary sat still in the house.

²¹Then said Martha unto Jesus, Lord, if thou hadst been here, my brother had not died.

²²But I know, that even now, whatsoever thou wilt ask of God, God will give it thee.

²³Jesus saith unto her, Thy brother shall rise again.

²⁴Martha saith unto him, I know that he shall rise again in the resurrection at the last day.

²⁵Jesus said unto her, I am the resurrection, and the life: he that believeth in me, though he were dead, yet shall he live:

²⁶And whosoever liveth and believeth in me shall never die. **Believest thou this?**

²⁷She saith unto him, Yea, Lord: I believe that thou art the Christ, the Son of God, which should come into the world.

²⁸And when she had so said, she went her way, and called Mary her sister secretly, saying, The Master is come, and calleth for thee.

²⁹As soon as she heard that, she arose quickly, and came unto him.

³⁰Now Jesus was not yet come into the town, but was in that place where Martha met him.

³¹The Jews then which were with her in the house, and comforted her, when they saw Mary, that she rose up hastily and went out, followed her, saying, She goeth unto the grave to weep there.

³²Then when Mary was come where Jesus was, and saw him, she fell down at his feet, saying unto him, Lord, if thou hadst been here, my brother had not died.

³³When Jesus therefore saw her weeping, and the Jews also weeping which came with her, he groaned in the spirit, and was troubled.

³⁴And said, Where have ye laid him? They said unto him, Lord, come and see.

³⁵Jesus wept.

³⁶Then said the Jews, Behold how he loved him!

³⁷And some of them said, Could not this man, which opened the eyes of the blind, have caused that even this man should not have died?

³⁸Jesus therefore again groaning in himself cometh to the grave. It was a cave, and a stone lay upon it.

³⁹Jesus said, Take ye away the stone. Martha, the sister of him that was dead, saith unto him, Lord, by this time he stinketh: for he hath been dead four days.

⁴⁰Jesus saith unto her, Said I not unto thee, that, if thou wouldest believe, thou shouldest see the glory of God?

⁴¹Then they took away the stone from the place where the dead was laid. And Jesus lifted up his eyes, and said, Father, I thank thee that thou hast heard me.

⁴²And I knew that thou hearest me always: but because of the people which stand by I said it, that they may believe that thou hast sent me.

⁴³And when he thus had spoken, he cried with a loud voice, Lazarus, come forth.

⁴⁴And he that was dead came forth, bound hand and foot with grave clothes: and his face was bound about with a napkin. Jesus saith unto them, Loose him, and let him go.

⁴⁵Then many of the Jews which came to Mary, and had seen the things which Jesus did, believed on him.

⁴⁶But some of them went their ways to the Pharisees, and told them what things Jesus had done.

⁴⁷Then gathered the chief priests and the Pharisees a council, and said, What do we? for this man doeth many miracles.

⁴⁸If we let him thus alone, all men will believe on him: and the Romans shall come and take away both our place and nation.

⁴⁹And one of them, named Caiaphas, being the high priest that same year, said unto them, Ye know nothing at all,

⁵⁰Nor consider that it is expedient for us, that one man should die for the people, and that the whole nation perish not.

⁵¹And this spake he not of himself: but being high priest that year, he prophesied that Jesus should die for that nation;

⁵²And not for that nation only, but that also he should gather together in one the children of God that were scattered abroad.

⁵³Then from that day forth they took counsel together for to put him to death.

⁵⁴Jesus therefore walked no more openly among the Jews; but went thence unto a country near to the wilderness, into a city called Ephraim, and there continued with his disciples.

⁵⁵And the Jews' passover was nigh at hand: and many went out of the country up to Jerusalem before the passover, to purify themselves.

⁵⁶Then sought they for Jesus, and spake among themselves, as they stood in the temple, What think ye, that he will not come to the feast?

⁵⁷Now both the chief priests and the Pharisees had given a commandment, that, if any man knew where he were, he should shew it, that they might take him.

The Death of Lazarus

11 Now a man named Lazarus was sick. He was from Bethany, the village of Mary and her sister Martha. ²(This Mary, whose brother Lazarus now lay sick, was the same one who poured perfume on the Lord and wiped his feet with her hair.) ³So the sisters sent word to Jesus, "Lord, the one you love is sick."

⁴When he heard this, Jesus said, "This sickness will not end in death. No, it is for God's glory so that God's Son may be glorified through it." ⁵Now Jesus loved Martha and her sister and Lazarus. ⁶So when he heard that Lazarus was sick, he stayed where he was two more days, ⁷and then he said to his disciples, "Let us go back to Judea."

⁸"But Rabbi," they said, "a short while ago the Jews there tried to stone you, and yet you are going back?"

⁹Jesus answered, "Are there not twelve hours of daylight? Anyone who walks in the daytime will not stumble, for they see by this world's light. ¹⁰It is when a person walks at night that they stumble, for they have no light."

¹¹After he had said this, he went on to tell them, "Our friend Lazarus has fallen asleep; but I am going there to wake him up."

¹²His disciples replied, "Lord, if he sleeps, he will get better." ¹³Jesus had been speaking of his death, but his disciples thought he meant natural sleep.

¹⁴So then he told them plainly, "Lazarus is dead, ¹⁵and for your sake I am glad I was not there, so that you may believe. But let us go to him."

¹⁶Then Thomas (also known as Didymus) said to the rest of the disciples, "Let us also go, that we may die with him."

Jesus Comforts the Sisters of Lazarus

¹⁷On his arrival, Jesus found that Lazarus had already been in the tomb for four days. ¹⁸Now Bethany was less than two miles from Jerusalem, ¹⁹and many Jews had come to Martha and Mary to comfort them in the loss of

their brother. 20When Martha heard that Jesus was coming, she went out to meet him, but Mary stayed at home.

21"Lord," Martha said to Jesus, "if you had been here, my brother would not have died. 22But I know that even now God will give you whatever you ask."

23Jesus said to her, "Your brother will rise again."

24Martha answered, "I know he will rise again in the resurrection at the last day."

25Jesus said to her, "I am the resurrection and the life. The one who believes in me will live, even though they die; 26and whoever lives by believing in me will never die. Do you believe this?"

27"Yes, Lord," she replied, "I believe that you are the Messiah, the Son of God, who is to come into the world."

28After she had said this, she went back and called her sister Mary aside. "The Teacher is here," she said, "and is asking for you." 29When Mary heard this, she got up quickly and went to him. 30Now Jesus had not yet entered the village, but was still at the place where Martha had met him. 31When the Jews who had been with Mary in the house, comforting her, noticed how quickly she got up and went out, they followed her, supposing she was going to the tomb to mourn there.

32When Mary reached the place where Jesus was and saw him, she fell at his feet and said, "Lord, if you had been here, my brother would not have died."

33When Jesus saw her weeping, and the Jews who had come along with her also weeping, he was deeply moved in spirit and troubled. 34"Where have you laid him?" he asked.

"Come and see, Lord," they replied.

35Jesus wept.

36Then the Jews said, "See how he loved him!"

37But some of them said, "Could not he who opened the eyes of the blind man have kept this man from dying?"

Jesus Raises Lazarus From the Dead

[38]Jesus, once more deeply moved, came to the tomb. It was a cave with a stone laid across the entrance. [39]"Take away the stone," he said.

"But, Lord," said Martha, the sister of the dead man, "by this time there is a bad odor, for he has been there four days."

[40]Then Jesus said, "Did I not tell you that if you believe, you will see the glory of God?"

[41]So they took away the stone. Then Jesus looked up and said, "Father, I thank you that you have heard me. [42]I knew that you always hear me, but I said this for the benefit of the people standing here, that they may believe that you sent me."

[43]When he had said this, Jesus called in a loud voice, "Lazarus, come out!" [44]The dead man came out, his hands and feet wrapped with strips of linen, and a cloth around his face.

Jesus said to them, "Take off the grave clothes and let him go."

The Plot to Kill Jesus

[45]Therefore many of the Jews who had come to visit Mary, and had seen what Jesus did, believed in him. [46]But some of them went to the Pharisees and told them what Jesus had done. [47]Then the chief priests and the Pharisees called a meeting of the Sanhedrin.

"What are we accomplishing?" they asked. "Here is this man performing many signs. [48]If we let him go on like this, everyone will believe in him, and then the Romans will come and take away both our temple and our nation."

[49]Then one of them, named Caiaphas, who was high priest that year, spoke up, "You know nothing at all! [50]You do not realize that it is better for you that one man die for the people than that the whole nation perish."

[51]He did not say this on his own, but as high priest that year he prophesied that Jesus would die for the Jewish nation, [52]and not only for that nation but also for the scattered children of God, to bring them together and make them one. [53]So from that day on they plotted to take his life.

[54] Therefore Jesus no longer moved about publicly among the people of Judea. Instead he withdrew to a region near the wilderness, to a village called Ephraim, where he stayed with his disciples.

[55] When it was almost time for the Jewish Passover, many went up from the country to Jerusalem for their ceremonial cleansing before the Passover. [56] They kept looking for Jesus, and as they stood in the temple courts they asked one another, "What do you think? Isn't he coming to the festival at all?" [57] But the chief priests and the Pharisees had given orders that anyone who found out where Jesus was should report it so that they might arrest him.

MARTHA

Abiding Faith, Fortitude, Instructed by Christ

Question	Answer
The heroine of this degree differs from the first 3 heroines in what respect?	Martha is the 1st of the heroines to be taken from the New Testament.
What was Martha's Family and home noted for?	Hospitality and restfulness
What was the name of the town where Martha lived?	Bethany
Martha's hometown was near what well-known hill or mountain?	Mount of Olives
How many composed Martha's family?	Three
What was Martha's husband named?	Simon
What was Martha's father named?	Joab
What great misfortune struck in Martha's home?	Her brother Lazarus died.
Was Martha's brother Lazarus the same Lazarus that was mentioned in the story of Luke 16:20?	No, the Lazarus mentioned in Luke 16:19-25 is a character in a parable.
In what book of the Bible is the story of Martha found?	The Gospel according to St. John, the 11th Chapter.
When did Jesus return to Bethany?	The 3rd hour of the 4th day after the entombment of Lazarus.
How long had Lazarus been dead when Jesus raised him?	Four Days (St. John 11:39)
The shortest verse in the Bible is found in this story. What is it?	Jesus wept. (St. John 11:35)
What is the Star Point Emblem of this degree?	The broken column.

What is the Pentagon Emblem of this degree?	The Lamb and the Cross
What does the broken column symbolize?	The untimely death of Lazarus
What figure is used in making the Sign for this degree?	Triangle
What does the sign signify?	The Divinity of Christ
The color of this degree signifies what?	Eternal Life
What is the floral emblem of this degree?	The Fern
What word is appropriate for this degree?	Immortality
What is the appropriate word for this degree?	Faith
What season of the year does Martha signify?	Winter
What is Martha's Jewel?	The Emerald
What does the name Martha signify?	Fortitude and Abiding Faith
What is the emblem for Christ in this degree?	The Lamb (The Matchless of God)
What is one of the symbolisms of green?	Green is the color of the ever-quickening covering of nature.
What does the broken Column remind one of?	That our hour of deepest sorrow and loneliness can be enlightened by the highest graces of God.
Who spoke the words that make up the pass of this degree?	Christ (St. John 11:26)
What lesson does this degree teach us?	To have unwavering faith in the hours of trial.

MARTHA

Martha is the Fourth Star Point Heroine

REPRESENTS

Martha represents the Ideal Sister. Martha assumed the responsibility for the care and comfort of her brother, Lazarus, and her sister, Mary, in their parentless home. Her devoted sisterly love for her brother contributed to the circumstances that led to the resurrection of Lazarus by Christ.

THE MEANING OF THE NAME

The name "MARTHA" means "Fortitude," "Abiding," and "Instructed by Christ." Martha had the fortitude to maintain her faith, even when her brother died, by abiding in the Word of God as she had been instructed by Christ.

COLOR

The vibrant deep green color of the springtime foliage is dedicated to Martha. Green the color of renewed life and growth, is the symbol of the new life which is eternal for all men through Christ.

FLOWER

The fern is dedicated to Martha because its endless greenness is symbolic of the endlessness of eternal life.

IDEALS

The ideals of Martha are Faith, Belief in Eternal Life, and Faith in the Immorality of the Soul. We can strive to achieve these ideals in our lives by so familiarizing ourselves with the Word of God and the Life Teachings of Jesus Christ that our eternal life may become as unshakeable as was the faith of Martha.

EMBLEMS

The emblem of Martha is the Broken Column. Martha's faith in God's promise of Eternal Life, through faith in Christ remained constant even when her brother's life, like a broken column, was broken off by mortal death. Therefore, the Broken Column is the emblem of sustaining power of faith in eternal life.

SYMBOL

The Lamb is the symbol of the story of Martha. Christ, the Lamb Slain for the sins of the world, raised Martha's brother from the dead as proof positive of the Power of God to bestow eternal life on all who would believe the Word in Christ the Son. One cannot mistake this challenge to maintain faith in the promise of the eternal life through belief in Jesus Christ.

JEWEL

The Emerald is the Jewel of Martha, because it representative of "Deathlessness".

SEASON

Martha represent the winter season because she represents knowledge that the winter of mortal life, or death, comes to all. It is then that Faith in Eternal Life is a force that will strengthen the individual so that he may face mortal death with calm and enter into eternal living with a peaceful heart and spirit.

BEATITUDE

The second beatitude is associated with Martha. "Blessed are they that mourn: for they shall be comforted." Matthew 5:4

THE STORY

John Chapter 11

Martha, Mary and Lazarus were friends of Jesus and lived in the city of Bethany, a little city which lie at the foot of the Mount of Olives. Christ had often been a visitor in their home. He often stopped at their simple home to rest and eat. Martha, being aware of Christ's interest and concern for every human problem whether great or small took her concerns to Jesus.

Read --- John Chapter 11

147

Story of
Electa

Electa

Definition	The Elect Lady (Oversees or called of God)
Degree	Mother
Gem	Ruby
Flower	Red Rose
Teaching	Fervent
Emblem	Cup
Color	Red
Beatitude	8th Beatitude (Matthew 5:11)
Verse Reference	11 John
Song	Jesus Keep Me Near the Cross
Season	Fall
Pass	Love One Another

ELECTA

5th POINT OF THE STAR

Degree	Mother
Meaning	Honorable called of God
Color	Red
Flower	Red Rose
Emblem	Cup
Symbol	Lion

PASS
Love one another?
(Spoken by John the Apostle)

BEATITUDE
Blessed are they which are persecuted for righteousness sake for theirs is the kingdom of heaven.

JEWEL
Ruby

SEASON
Autumn

ELECTA

The Elect Lady

The scene of the fifth Star Point is laid in Asia Minor, a peninsula lying between the Black Sea on the north and the Mediterranean Sea on the south. On the west coast of the peninsula in Lydian, near the mouth of the Cayster river, situated on high ground of a fertile plain, is Ephesus, the residence of Saint John from about 67

A.D. to the end of his life. Except for occasional visits to established churches in Asia Minor, St. John most probably rarely went out from Ephesus. Asia Minor is a region of extraordinary fertility and beauty, but has bee ruined by centuries of waste and misgovernment The exact date of the writing of the Epistle is not known, but is placed between 85 - 95 A.D.

Our information concerning Electa is based, for the most part on Masonic tradition. She was born and brought up in Asia Minor and, naturally, reared under the principles of paganism. She seems to have been well advanced in years when the edict of the Roman Government was issued against the followers of Christ. It is quite apparent that she was converted to the Christian faith under the preaching of St Paul. Furthermore, she appears to have been a very influential woman in her community. She apparently spent her income in relieving the poor; devoted much time to the care of them and kept open house for the indigent and hungry travelers. Benevolence seems to have been the great passion of her life - she sought out those who were lost and ministered to them.

The Christian religion, as we have endeavored to make clear, had become quite obnoxious to the people, and pressure was brought upon the Roman government for some action. Electa's mansion was said to have been the most splendid in the province. The edict of the Roman Government was issued against everyone who professed the religion of Christ All Christians were bound to renounce it under penalty of death.

Soldiers were enjoined to execute the law without mercy. All those suspected of holding the Christian faith were commanded to trample upon the cross that was handed to them as a testimony of their renunciation. Electa absolutely refused to comply with the edict. She spumed the test and said that she would never renounce her religion. She and her family were forthwith cast in.to a dungeon for twelve months, at the end of which time the judge appeared and offered her another opportunity to recant from Christianity, and again she refused. Thereupon she was dragged forth and savagely scourged nigh to death. They were then taken in oxcarts to the nearest hill where she and her family, one by one, were nailed to the cross. She was the last of the family to be crucified, and thus witnessed the tragic

151

death of her husband and children. She may well have uttered with her expiring breath, "Father, forgive them, for they know not what they do."

She professed her faith to the whole world, although she knew what reproaches, persecutions even unto death that she must undergo for the stand that she took. It meant the loss of good name, wealth, of means of doing good, of liberty, of husband and children, and of life itself. Yet she was willing to undergo all these things for the love of Christ and for the Christian religion in which she showed the most implicit faith. What a rich heritage is hers! "For we know that if our earthly house of the tabernacle were dissolved, we have a building of God, a house not made with hands, eternal in the heavens."

-Some Further info on Electa -

Why do we refer to Electa as the Mother? Why do we use the color Red to represent Mother? Where did the symbol of Electa, the Lion, originate? And the Cup?

Of all the Star Points, most of us probably know less of the story of Electa than any of the others. Was she a real live person or a symbolic representation of Christians everywhere?

Here we will try and understand some of the story as written and even more that has been handed down as tradition through the centuries.

Sign of the Mother: Cross the arms over the breast, the left arm over the right, and the ends of the fingers on the shoulders.

Cast eyes upward.

Pass: " Love one another!" A member on seeing the Mother's sign should respond with these words.

ELECTA

Her gentle smile and yielding heart
Shall grace our world no more;
She chose the true but bitter part
Her Savior chose before;
The Cross its gloomy load had borne,
The grave concealed its prey,
But in the triumphs she had won
He cast all fear away.
This heartless world but ill can spare
Its jewels rich and few, --
But she, most excellent and rare,
The generous and the true –
She, is departing, left to earth
Such patterns of her faith,
That though her life was matchless worth
Even worthier was her death.
But her we learn, the tenderest heart
Is bravest to endure –
For at the Cross He'll not desert
Who all its sufferings bore;
Amongst ten thousand, fairest she,
When bleeding, dying, high
Her risen Lord proclaimed her free,
And called her to the sky.
Her fame upon the wings of Time
Through every land has swept, --
Electa's FAITH, unmatched, sublime,
Electa's NAME has kept;
Meek, radiant one! Whose willing blood
Thy faith in Christ did seal,
While hears can feel and tears be stirred,
Thy history we will tell.

-Rob Morris

TO ELECTA
"Hospitality"

The beautiful hands of our Mother
Breaking bread, to serve each friend;
His lovely smile, in passing the Cup
Are treasures time never will end.
Electa, our Lady of warm charity,
And hospitality, true,
Fills her Cup with sincere love,
To be shared by me, and you.
Close to the glowing heart of our Star,
And that of each sister and brother,
Is the sweet counsel Electa gives,
"Let s love one another."
Her message comes to each member
With gladness, deep and sincere;
Walking together the Star-lit trail
We grow closer, year by year!

153

2 John King James Version (KJV)

¹The elder unto the elect lady and her children, whom I love in the truth; and not I only, but also all they that have known the truth;

²For the truth's sake, which dwelleth in us, and shall be with us for ever.

³Grace be with you, mercy, and peace, from God the Father, and from the Lord Jesus Christ, the Son of the Father, in truth and love.

⁴I rejoiced greatly that I found of thy children walking in truth, as we have received a commandment from the Father.

⁵And now I beseech thee, lady, not as though I wrote a new commandment unto thee, but that which we had from the beginning, that we **love one another.**

⁶And this is love, that we walk after his commandments. This is the commandment, That, as ye have heard from the beginning, ye should walk in it.

⁷For many deceivers are entered into the world, who confess not that Jesus Christ is come in the flesh. This is a deceiver and an antichrist.

⁸Look to yourselves, that we lose not those things which we have wrought, but that we receive a full reward.

⁹Whosoever transgresseth, and abideth not in the doctrine of Christ, hath not God. He that abideth in the doctrine of Christ, he hath both the Father and the Son.

¹⁰If there come any unto you, and bring not this doctrine, receive him not into your house, neither bid him God speed:

¹¹For he that biddeth him God speed is partaker of his evil deeds.

¹²Having many things to write unto you, I would not write with paper and ink: but I trust to come unto you, and speak face to face, that our joy may be full.

¹³The children of thy elect sister greet thee. Amen.

2 John New International Version (NIV)

[1]The elder,

To the lady chosen by God and to her children, whom I love in the truth—and not I only, but also all who know the truth— [2]because of the truth, which lives in us and will be with us forever:

[3]Grace, mercy and peace from God the Father and from Jesus Christ, the Father's Son, will be with us in truth and love.

[4]It has given me great joy to find some of your children walking in the truth, just as the Father commanded us. [5]And now, dear lady, I am not writing you a new command but one we have had from the beginning. I ask that we love one another. [6]And this is love: that we walk in obedience to his commands. As you have heard from the beginning, his command is that you walk in love.

[7]I say this because many deceivers, who do not acknowledge Jesus Christ as coming in the flesh, have gone out into the world. Any such person is the deceiver and the antichrist. [8]Watch out that you do not lose what we[c] have worked for, but that you may be rewarded fully. [9]Anyone who runs ahead and does not continue in the teaching of Christ does not have God; whoever continues in the teaching has both the Father and the Son. [10]If anyone comes to you and does not bring this teaching, do not take them into your house or welcome them. [11]Anyone who welcomes them shares in their wicked work.

[12]I have much to write to you, but I do not want to use paper and ink. Instead, I hope to visit you and talk with you face to face, so that our joy may be complete.

[13]The children of your sister, who is chosen by God, send their greetings.

ELECTA

Called of God; Overseer

QUESTIONS	ANSWERS
What does the name Electa signify?	Called by God/Lady
What biblical Book refers to Electa?	Second Epistle of John
Is the story of Electa a biblical story?	No
In the biblical reference to Electa, she is called what?	Elect Lady
What was Electa most noted for?	Hospitality & Love
Who admonished Electa to continue in the commandment: "Love One Another"?	John the Apostle
What makes Electa outstanding among women?	She suffered death rather than deny Christ.
How did Electa and her family meet their death?	They were crucified.
What is another name for Electa's degree?	Mother
What is the virtue attached to this degree?	Fervency, Hospitality and Love
What is the Pentagon symbol signify?	Lion
What does the Pentagon symbol signify?	Power & Strength
What season of the year does Electa represent?	Autumn
What 3 things does the color of this degree symbolize?	Blood, Wine & Fire
What does blood symbolize?	Life is sacrifice
What does fire represent?	Purification
What is wine emblematic of?	The Spirit
The cup is a symbol of what?	Human Body
The Cup denotes what?	Plenty – The Life Principle
What figure is used in making the sign of this degree?	A Pentagon

What do the sides of this figure represent?	The Five senses
What does the Heart represent in this Sign?	The Altar
What is the Christ symbol in this degree?	Tribe of Judah
What symbol represents Strength and Power?	Lion
What jewel is dedicated to Electa?	Ruby
What is the Star Point Emblem of this degree?	Cup
What is the flower of this degree?	Red Rose
What does the flower symbolize?	Love
What are Electa's Ideals?	Love & Hospitality
What is Electa's beatitude?	8th Beatitude/Matthew 5:10

Test
yourself

Adah

1. What is Adah's season?
2. What is Adah's beatitude?
3. What does her color mean?
4. What is her Christ like symbol?
5. Who was Adah's father?
6. What judge was Adah's father?
7. What is her pass?
8. What is her jewel?
9. Did Adah go up to the mountains alone? With whom did she go with?
10.   What was Adah's Grandfather name?

Open discuss notes:

RUTH

WHAT DOES THE SHEAF OF GRAIN TEACHES US?

WHAT WAS THE ORIGINAL FLOWER DEDICATED TO RUTH?

WHAT DO THE HISTORICAL PERIODS OF THE STORIES OF RUTH AND ADAH HAVE IN COMMON?

WHO WAS BOAZ?

WHAT WAS NAOMI'S HUSBAND'S NAME?

HOW DID NAOMI AND HER HUSBAND COME TO LIVE IN MOAB?

WHAT FAMILY CONNECTION WAS THERE BETWEEN NAOMI AND BOAZ?

WHAT IS YELLOW EMBLEMATIC OF?

WHAT DOES THE JASMINE TEACH US?

DID NAOMI WORSHIP IDOL GOD WHILE SHE LIVED IN MOAB?

WHAT ARE THE TWO KINDS OF JASMINES?

WHAT DOES THE WORD "GLEAN" MEAN?

WHAT FLOWER BESIDES THE JASMINE IS DEDICATED TO RUTH?

WHAT IS THE VIRTURE STRESSED BY THIS DEGREE?

WHAT TIME OF YEAR DID RUTH AND NAOMI ARRIVE IN BETHLEHEM?

WERE ANY CHILDREN BORN TO RUTH AND BOAZ?

WHAT WAS THE NAME OF RUTH'S FIRST HUSBAND?

NAOMI TOLD HER FRIENDS IN BETHLEHEM TO CALL HER WHAT?

WHERE DID RUTH SPEND HER EARLY LIFE?

WHAT DOES THE COLOR YELLOW SYMBOLIZE?

WHAT FLOWER AT PRESENT IS DEDICATED TO RUTH?

FOR WHAT WILL RUTH ALWAYS BR REMEMBERED?

WHAT DOES THE STORY OF RUTH TEACHES US?

WHAT DID RUTH DO FOR A LIVING IN HER NEW HOME?

WHAT DOES THIS DEGREE TEACH US?

WHAT SEASON OF THE YEAR DOES RUTH REPESENT?

THE LILY OF THE VALLEY IS ASSOCIATED WITH WHAT?

WHO SAID: " ENTREAT ME NOT TO LEAVE THEE"

WHAT IS THE PENTAGON SYMBOL FOR THIS DEGREE?

WHAT IS THE CHRIST SYMBOL OF THIS DREGEE?

WHAT KIND OF GRAIN COMPOSES THE SHEAF OF GRAIN?

WHAT DOES THE NAME MEAN?

HOW WAS THE MARRIAGE OF RUTH AND BOAZ MADE POSSIBLE?

WHERE WAS RUTH'S ORINIGAL HOME?

WHAT DOES THE NAME RUTH STANDS FOR?

HOW DID RUTH MEET BOAZ?

WHAT IS RUTH'S JEWEL?

WHO WAS ORPAH?

BY WHAT OTHER NAME IS THIS DEGREE KNOWN?

WHAT DID THE MAOBITES WORSHIP?

WHY DID RUTH LEAVE HOME?

RUTH WAS A DESCENDANT OF WHOM?

ESTHER

IN WHAT COUNTRY DID THE STORY OF ESTHER TAKE PLACE?

WHY WAS THE FIRST QUWWN DIVORCED AND BANISHED FROM THE PALACE?

HOW DID THE JEWS COME TO BE IN PERISA?

WHERE IS THE BOOK OF ESTHER TO BE FOUND IN THE BIBLE?

WHEN WAS ESTHER MADE QUEEN?

WHAT DID MOEDECAI SO WHEN HE LEARNED OF THE EDICT TO DESTROY THE JEWS?

WHAT IS THE SIGNIFICANCE OF THE SIGN OF THIS DEGREE?

WHAT FUTHER LESSON MAY BE LEARNED FROM THIS FLOWER?

WHAT DOES THE FLOWER TEACH?

WHAT DO THE CROWN AND SCEPTER REMIND US OF?

WHAT GREAT LESSON DOES THIS DEGREE TEACH?

WHY IS THE SUN AN APPROPRIATE EMBLEM FOR ESTHER?

ABOUT WHAT YEAR DID THE MAIN PART OF THE STORY TAKE PLACE?

164

BY WHAT OTHER NAME IS THE BIBLICAL AHASUERUS KNOW?

WHAT POSITION DID MORDECAI HOLD?

WHAT HAPPENED TO HAMAN?

WHO WAS HAMAN?

WHAT DOES THE NAME HADASSAH MEAN?

HOW LING WAS THE PREPARATION PERIOD FOR MADIES WHO WERE TO GO BRFORE THE KING?

WHAT MADE HAMAN SO ANGRY WITH MORDECAI?

WITH WHAT OTHER GREAT BIBLICAL CHARACTER CAN ESTHER BE COMPARED?

WHAT PRESENT DAY FEAST COMMEMORATES ESTHER'S VICTORY FOR HER PEOPLE?

THE COLOR OF THIS DEGREE IS SYMBOLIC OF WHAT?

WHAT DOES THE FLOWER OF THIS DEGREE STAND FOR?

WHAT ATTRIBUTE DOES THIS DEGREE TEACH US TO CULTIVATE?

THE DUAL SYMBOLS OF THE CROWN AND SCEPTER SIGNIFY WHAT?

WHAT WORD BLONGS TO THIS DEGREE?

165

MARTHA

THE HEROINE LOF THIS DEGREE DIFFERS FROM THE FIRST THREE HEROINE 'S IN WHAT RESPECT?

WHAT WAS MARTHA'S FAMILY AND HOME NOTED FOR?

WHAT WAS THE NAME OF THE TOWN WHERE MARTHA LIVED?

MARTHA'S HOME TOWN WAS NEAR WHAT WELL KNOWN HILL OR MOUNTAIN?

HOW MANY COMPOSED MARTHA'S FAMILY?

WHAT WAS MARTHA'S HUSBAND NAMED?

WHAT WAS MARTHA'S FATHER NAME?

WHAT GREAT MISFORTUNE STRUCK IN MARTHA'S HOME?

WAS MARTHA'S BROTHER LAZARUS THE SAME LAZARUS MENTIONED IN THE STORY OF LUKE 16:20?

IN WHAT BOOK OF THE BIBLE IS THE STORY OF MARTHA FOUND?

WHEN DID JESUS RETURN TO BETHANY?

HOW LONG HAD LAZARUS BEEN DEAD WHEN JESUS RAISED HIM?

THE SHORTEST VERSE IN THE BIBLE IS FOUND IN THIS STORY. WHAT IS IT?

WHAT IS THE STAR POINT EMBLEM IF THIS DEGREE?

WHAT IS THE PENTAGON EMBLEM OF THEIS DEGREE?

WHAT DOES THE PENTAGON EMBLEM SIGINFY?

WHAT FIGURE IS USED IN MAKING THE SIGN OF THIS DEGREE?

WHAT DIES THE SIGN SIGNIFY?

THE COLOR OF THIS DEGREE SYMBOLIZES WHAT?

WHAT IS THE FLORAL EMBLEM OF THIS DEGREE?

WHAT DOED THE FLORAL EMBLEM OF THIS DEGREE?

WHAT WORD IS APPROPRIATE FOR THIS DEGREE?

WHAT SEASON OF THE YEAR DOES MARTHA SIGNIFY?

WHAT IS MARTHA'S JEWEL?

WHAT DOES THE NAME MARTHA SIGNIFY?

WHAT IS THE EMBLEM FOR CHRIST IN THIS DEGREE?

WHAT IS ONE OF THE SYMBOLISMS OF THE TRIANGLE?

WHAT IS ONE OF THE SYMBOLIMS OF GREEN?

WHAT DOES THE BROKEN COLUMN REMIND ONE OF?

WHO SPOKE THE WORDS THAT MAKE UP THE PASS OF THIS DEGREE?

WHAT LESSON DOES THIS DEGREE TEACH US?

Electa

1. In the bible what name is referenced to her?
2. What is her flower?
3. What is her beatitude?
4. What does the heart represent in this sign?
5. Where can her story be found in the bible?
6. What degree is she?
7. What is her season?
8. What is the cup a symbol of?
9. Who wrote the letter to her?
10.   What happened to her family?

1. What year is associated with Martha?
2. What 2 positions share the same Jewel?
3. What is a pentagon?
4. What is the year of establishment of the OES?
5. What 2 degrees does the Lily appear as an emblem?
6. What is the mission of the order?
7. Who was Othneil?
8. How the marriage of Ruth and Boaz was made possible?
9. Calling up an officer requires how many raps of the gavel?
10. What does AF & AM stand for?
11. What 3 things does the color "Red" symbolizes for Electa?
12. What is the 2nd landmark?
13. Give me one of each representation of 3-5-7?
14. What does the name Hadassah mean?
15. What are the primary colors in the Order of Eastern Star?
16. What figure is used in making the sign for Martha degree?
17. What are the 3 steps in becoming an Eastern Star?
18. The Jasper is the jewel of what officer?
19. Who saved the ancestral line of Mordecai?
20. The equilateral triangle that the order is based on is?

Bonus: How can you prove you are a member of the order?

Setting up the chapter room

Name:

1. How many chairs sets up a complete chapter room?

2. How many trustees do we have?

3. How many star points do we have?

4. How many flags do we have?

5. Who sits in the South?

6. What seat is in front of the west?

7. What seat is in front of the Secretary?

8. Who sit by the door?

9. Who can walk around the chapter room without getting a fine?

10. My seat is between the Marshall and trustee?

Bonus: Which two people in the chapter holds the same jewel?

FILL IN THE BLANK

1. Where do violets bloom? _____

2. What is Adah's Christ-like symbol? _____

3. How long had Lazarus been dead before Jesus raised him? _____

4. How many feasts did Esther prepare for the king in order to save her people? _____

5. Who is Electa's pentagon symbol? _____

6. What was the original flower dedicated to Ruth? _____

7. What is Martha's season? _____

8. Adah lifted her veil to signify her _____

9. What is the Order dedicated to? _____

10. What represents God and Eternity both having neither beginning nor end? _____

11. What is the virtue associated with the Widow's degree? _____

12. How many animals are on the signet and name them. _____

13. Who did Jephthah wage war against? _____

14. The shortest verse in the Bible is found in the story of Martha. What is it?

    _____

15. The pass of the Heroine that represents the Mother's degree is _____

THE NAME GAME

16. What does the name "Esther" Mean? _____

17. Who were Boaz's parents? _____

18. Esther's original name was _____

19. What does "Electa" mean? _____

20. Name Mara's husband and her 2 sons. _____

    _____

21. Jephthah's father's name was _____

22. What 2 heroines were not specifically named in the bible? _____

23. Who was Abihail's daughter? _____

24. Martha and her family lived near what well know hill or mountain? _____

25. Jephthah's mother was a (use biblical terms)_____

Bonus Question: Name at least 6 of the 13 Judges: _____

_____

_____

Name: _____ Chapter: _____

OES
Glossary

OES GLOSSARY
OF
ABREVIATIONS

Affiliations/Degrees

OES	Order of Eastern Star
QoS	Queen of the South
OoA	Order o Amaranth
HoJ	Heroines of Jericho
DoS	Daughters of the Sphinx
F & AM	Free and Accepted Masons ("3 letter")
AF & AM	Ancient Free and Accepted Masons ("4 letter")

Grand Chapter Officers

MGWM	Most Worshipful Grand Master
MEGP	Most Eminent Grand Patron
MWGM	Most Worthy Grand Matron
GAP	Grand Associate Patron
GAM	Grand Associate Matron
GFS	Grand Financial Secretary
GRS	Grand Recording Secretary
GT	Grand Treasurer
GC	Grand Conductress
GAC	Grand Associate Conductress

Subordinate Chapter Officers

WM	Worthy Matron
WP	Worthy Patron
PWM	Past Worthy Matron
AM	Associate Matron
AP	Associate Patron
FS	Financial Secretary
RS	Recording Secretary
TR	Treasurer
CON	Conductress
AC	Associate Conductress

OES GLOSSARY
OF
WORDS AND PHRASES

Adoptive Rite	Made or acquired by adoption
Ballot	The action or system of secret voting
Business Meeting – Monthly	Meeting in which Chapter business is conducted
Called or Special Meeting	Meeting called by Chapter to discuss pressing/important issues
Candidate	Female who has been voted on and accepted into Chapter while initiating
Chapter	Female group in the Order of Eastern Star
Dimit	exit from a chapter for reasons up to and including unfavorable removal or demotion in instances of an un-6.nancial status, behavior unbecoming of an Eastern Star, insubordination or simply at one's own request having nothing to do with any of the aforementioned reasons
Due(s)	Assessments paid to subordinate chapters by each active and financial member on the roster. Dues are typically used for the assistance of the chapter, up to and including; (1) payment of registration for any Grand Chapter event, (2) assistance of financial distress with a Sister within the Chapter, (3) expenses for Chapter Officers who travel on official OES business, (4) petty cash for fundraising events, (S)funds for community service events, etc.
Etiquette	The conduct or procedure required by good breeding or prescribed by authority to be observed in social or official life
Fines	Monetary fee(s) issued as a result of not following guidelines set forth in the Chapter's
By-Laws	(see page five (5) of the chapter by-laws for further explanation)
Grand Chapter Application	Application made to the Grand Chapter for affiliation
Install/Installation Ceremony	To induct into an office, rank, or order (ceremony)
Labyrinth	A place constructed of or full of intricate passageways and blind alleys
Lodge	Male equivalent to a female chapter
Parliamentary Law	The rules and precedents governing the proceedings of deliberative assemblies and other organizations

Pentagram	Figure made up of five sides, representing the five races of humanity.
Petitioner	Female who has made application and has not been voted on during initiation
Proclamation/Summons	An official, formal public announcement
Protocol	The code prescribing strict adherence to correct etiquette and precedence
Quorum	Legal number of people it takes to hold a meeting, vote
Regalia	Garments, emblems, symbols, paraphernalia that make up the OES wardrobe
Signet	A seal used officially to give personal authority to a document in lieu of signature
Star	Star of Bethlehem
Subordinate Chapter Application	Application made to local chapter for affiliation
Tax	Monies assessed by the Grand Chapter, to be paid by each active, financial member, for Education, Building fund, Congress, General, Charity and Annual.
Un-Financial-Status	That is the result of being two or more months past due in paying your dues to your subordinate chapter.

OES GLOSSARY
OF
CHAPTER POSITIONS

Worthy Matron

The duties of the **Worthy Matron** shall be to open and preside over the Chapter during its deliberations, to see that the by-laws are promptly enforced, that the returns of the work of the chapter are made annually to the Grand Chapter, and that the purposes of the Chapter are properly accomplished. She shall oversee all study sessions and is responsible for the Chapters continuous learning of the Order. The Worthy Matron may, at times, appoint another member to preside or teach during a chapter study session. In the event of the dissolution of the Chapter, she shall promptly deliver all the Records, Books, Warrants, Rituals, etc. to the Grand Secretary for preservation.

Worthy Patron

The **Worthy Patron** (or a Master Mason recommended by the Worthy Patron) is to preside during the ceremony of initiation, and at the election and installation of officers, to assist the Worthy Matron in the performance of her duties, and to have supervisory care over the affairs of the Chapter.

Past Worthy Matron

The **Past Worthy Matron** shall council the Worthy Matron in the discharge of her duties. She shall also serve as Chair of the Community Service Committee and/or Fundraiser Committee.

Associate Matron

The **Associate Matron** shall assist the Worthy Matron in the discharge of her duties and in the absence of the latter, shall preside and assume all the responsibilities of that office.

Associate Patron

The **Associate Patron** (or a Master Mason recommended by the Worthy Patron) In the absence of the Worthy Matron will preside during the ceremony of initiation, and at the election and installation of officers, to assist the Worthy Patron in the performance of his duties. In addition, he may work together with the Associate Matron In the education of the Five Points of the Star (optional).

Treasurer

The **Treasurer** shall receive all monies, deposit the same in her name as Treasurer In a bank selected by the members, keep a just and regular account thereof, and pay out the same by order of the Worthy Matron and Secretary, with the consent of the Chapter. She shall report monthly to the Chapter the amount of her receipts and expenditures by item. At the expiration of her term, she shall deliver all money, books, papers, receipts, checking account information, and other property belonging of the Chapter to her successor in office.

Financial Secretary

The **Financial Secretary** shall keep financial record of all dues, taxes and/or assessments for the Chapter. Collect monies at meetings and issues receipts, inform all members of the amount of their indebtedness and perform such other duties as may be required of her by the Worthy Matron of the Chapter. At the expiration of her term of office, she shall deliver books, papers, and other property belonging to the chapter, to her successor in office.

Recording Secretary

The **Recording Secretary** shall record the proceedings of the Chapter and keep an accurate account between the Chapter and its members. She shall also issues notices and summons for meetings, read correspondence and renders a complete statement of the labor of the Chapter to the Grand Secretary of the Grand Chapter. She shall keep a register of all the members of the Chapter, notify all committees of the appointment and perform such other duties as may be required of her by the Worthy Matron of the Chapter. At the expiration of her term of office, she shall deliver books, papers, and other property belonging to the chapter, to her successor in office.

Conductress

The **Conductress** shall receive and conduct all candidates through the ceremonies of the order. She is also responsible for setting up and breaking down the Chapter room in preparation of formal meetings.

Associate Conductress

The **Associate Conductress** shall be in charge of the preparation of candidates for ceremonies of the Order, assist the Conductress in her duties, and perform such duties as ascertained to her office and as may be required by the Matron and Conductress. She is also responsible for the set up and breakdown of the Chapter room after formal meetings.

Five Points of the Star - The Heroines

The **Heroines - Adah, Ruth, Esther, Martha, and Electa** shall perform such duties as are required by the Ritual of the Order, under the direction of the Worthy Matron. In addition, serve on the Sick and Distress Committee along with the Associate Matron.

Warder/Sentinel

The **Warder/Sentinel** shall guard the door from the inside and outside, report all persons requesting admission, and see that none enter except such that have been duly vouched for. The Marshal shall answer for each member when roll is being called.

Marshal

The **Marshal** is the only person allowed to move around the room while meetings are in. session. The Marshal is also responsible for the giving of the signs during the opening ceremonies of the Business meeting. The Marshal shall serve as the "armor bearer" to the Worthy Matron and assist her upon arrival and exit of the Chapter room.

Chaplain

The **Chaplain** shall perform the devotional exercises of the Chapter, except where otherwise stipulated in the Ritual of degrees. She shall also serve as spiritual liaison for Chapter members.

Board of Trustees

The **Board of Trustees** shall verify that all books and records of the Chapter are accurate and that the Chapter is running in. accordance with the By-laws of the Chapter and Grand Chapter. They will also be responsible for Chapter property. Board of Trustees is made up of the Chair of Trustees, Trustee (Secretary), Trustee (Treasurer).

Chairman of Trustees

The **Chairman of Trustees** for Charity Work will be responsible for searching and orchestrating all charity events for the Chapter while working under the Treasurer's tutelage.

Historian

The **Historian** shall record all Chapter events through film, video and is responsible for keeling a scrap book of Chapter events and proper storage and/or presentation of such items. She shall also be responsible for the Chapter's website in. the future.

Musician

The **Musician** is responsible for providing the musical enjoyment for the Chapter room during Business meetings; study sessions, Installation/Imitation Ceremonies and/or Chapter of Sorrow.

OES Flag Bearer

The **OES flag bearer** is responsible for ushering in the Order of Eastern Star flag during opening ceremonies and retiring it at closing ceremonies.

Christian Flag Bearer

The **Christian flag bearer** is responsible for ushering in the Christian flag during opening ceremonies and retiring it at closing ceremonies.

American Flag Bearer

The **American flag bearer** is responsible for ushering in. the American flag during opening ceremonies and retiring it at closing ceremonies.

OES GLOSSARY
OF
SUBORDINATE CHAPTER COMMITTEES

By-Laws

The By-Laws committee is made up of the Worthy Matron, Worthy Patron, Past Worthy Matron, Associate Matron, Associate Patron and Secretary of the Chapter. Responsibilities of the Committee are to author the laws of the Chapter. The Committee will meet twice a year to review the Laws and discuss any alterations, additions, deletions, etc. to the Laws, if needed.

Ways and Means/Fundraiser

Ways and Means: Will operate financially for the benefit of the Chapter and find ways to generate revenue.

Charity/ Community Service

Charity: It shall be the duty of this committee to collect donations for Charity when need be and announce the amount collected by them in open meeting, turn the same over to the Secretary to be recorded in the minutes and deposited by the Secretary or Treasurer.

Investigating

Investigating: Petitions for initiation or affiliation when received by the Chapter shall be referred to a committee of three (3), two (2) Sisters and one (1) Brother. This committee of the Worthy Patron, Associate Matron and Past Worthy Matron shall make due inquiry into the moral character and qualifications of the candidates and report at the next stated.

Relief and Distress

Relief and Distress: Associate Matron and the Five (5) Points of the Star.

Words Frequently Mispronounced

Actuate	Ack-chew-wait
Address	Uh-dress
Affiliate	Uh-fill-ee-ate
Amenable	Uh-men-uh-bull
Admonish	Add-mon-ish
Ammon	Am-mon
Ascertain	As-sir-tayn
Baton	Buh-toyn
Beneficent	Ben-ef-i-cent
Boaz	Bo-azz
Cabalistic	Cab-uh-lis-tik
Dais	Die-us
Edict	Eee-dict
Electa	E-leck-ta
Elimilech	E-lim-e-lecke
Effulgent	Ef-ful-jent
Inviolably	In-vi-ull-blee
Jephthah	Jef-tha
Jessamine	Jes-uh-mean
Labyrinth	Lab-eei-rinth
Moab	Moe-ab
Peculiar	Pee-cul-yur
Perpetual	Per-pet-u-ahl
Solemn	Sol-em
Solemnity	Sol-em-nuh-tee

Fun things to do

OES Points
circle the words

```
                    N  I
                    W  H
                 X  O  I  F
                 Z  R  S  R
              X  E  C  L  N  E
              H  W  O  P  S  E
A  E  T  I  H  W  Y  L  A  W  T  D  N  E  B  O  U  O  V  Y
J  B  I  L  A  T  A  F  A  H  O  M  M  L  R  W  I  D  O  W
   H  R  E  D  A  L  I  E  V  S  L  U  V  Z  G  P  R  M
      P  B  A  H  L  R  P  U  C  E  L  E  K  V  P  E
         B  H  T  B  R  O  K  E  N  O  E  Z  V  T
            V  R  N  Z  J  A  P  F  C  Q  Y  F
         X  X  A  O  X  R  D  T  A  M  S  P  I  U
         N  H  M  G  E  Y  B  E  C  W  O  T  W  H
         Q  T  R  E  T  S  I  S  R  P  E  I  T  A  V  J
         U  I  S  H  S  G  A     K  E  L  F  H  R  Z
      R  R  W  G  G  D  E        S  V  E  E  E  Y  A
      X  O  U  G  D              W  H  D  R  L
   J  R  A  R                       J  K  V  F
   D  D                                X  K
```

BROKEN	COLUMN	DAUGHTER
FATAL	MOTHER	SISTER
WHITE	YELLOW	BLUE
CUP	ESTHER	MARTHA
RUTH	SWORD	VEIL
WIFE	ADAH	CROWN
SCEPTER	ELECTA	GREEN
RED	STAR	WIDOW

183

Name:_____

Complete the crossword puzzle below

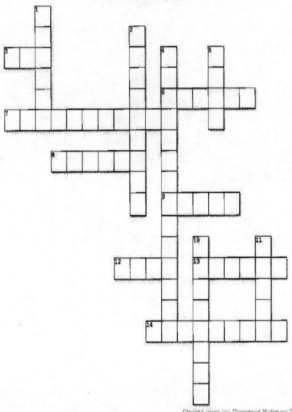

Created using the Crossword Maker on TheTeachersCorner.net

Across
3. equilateral triangles
6. Martha's season
7. scroll and baton
8. letter to john
9. adah, ruth, esther, martha, electa
12. Left Shoe
13. Persian Empire
14. central points of the star

Down
1. the 6th judge
2. emerald is my jewel
4. Adah's pass
5. What is Adah's color?
10. human body
11. the star spell

184

Knowing your points II

Write the name of the correct match next to each problem.

1. _____   a. Who is this

2. _____   b. letter from john

3. _____   c. veil

4. _____   d. left shoe

5. _____   e. lamb

6. _____   f. vashti

7. _____   g. yellow

8. _____   h. winter

9. _____   i. no season

10. _____   j. believeth thou this

11. _____   k. violets

12. _____   l. blessed are the pure in heart for they shall see God

13. _____   m. persian empire

14. _____   n. bitter draught

15. _____   o. overseer

16. _____   p. endurance

17. _____   q. feast

18. _____   r. mt. olives

19. _____   s. lion

20. _____   t. daddy was a judge

185

Know your Points
Please unscramble the words below

Created on TheTeachersCorner.net Scramble Maker

1. ylil

2. eLtf heSo

3. iveolst

4. ngere

5. eirndf ot usJse

6. ntfouiCccira

7. lEehmilec

8. enop lbebi

9. tsiavh

10. irbtte uhgdrta

11. ybuR

12. iVle

13. tamunu

14. nierspa eeimpr

15. rexsXe

16. reettl omrf onjh

17. mlba

18. ezhers

19. eErgvenre

20. lwoeyl

Points
Myra

These are the 5 Heroines of the Star!!!!

```
c r s r d e l i r l o n o f f
n e d d e o i t t h i u o d
m a h f w y e l l o w o c l e
u a i d d t v o m w r c s e o
l w m r r r d a e w y w e l b
o a o a e e n a r c b w t n o
c e t d m c a e u n e l e h t
n s h a i a d p t g o n h a e
e e e h f w r d h c t u t w h
k g r k h a o t h r o h w w k
o r e i e t w d h b l u e d h
r e t p e c s d n a n w o r c
b e s t h e r a w s f a a e e
a n i l s l r d h e d t n r e
c n s a g e d r r n e i a f d
```

adah	blue	broken column
crown and scepter	cup	daugther
electa	esther	fatal
green	martha	mother
red	ruth	sister
star	sword and veil	white
widow	wife	yellow

OES Crossword Puzzle

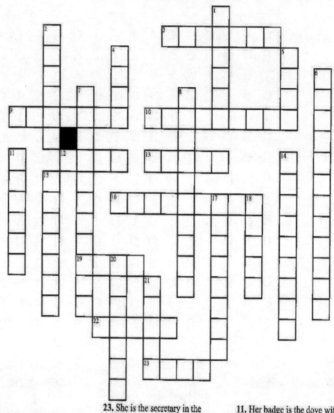

Across

3. Her duty is to respond to the roll call of officers

9. All of our signs are given in three...

10. The candidate is conducted through the mazy...

12. Her symbol is the open Bible

13. We've come this far by

16. It is the secret word in the Royal & Exalted Degree of the Amaranth

19. The Worthy Matron presides in the...

22. We have two of these, one is a general and the other is a special

23. She is the secretary in the Queen of the South Degree

Down

1. She becomes Princess Syene in the Q of the S degree

2. She is referred to the elect lady in 2 John

4. You'll hear five of these at the door

5. She is Naomi's daughter-n-law

6. His badge of office are the square & compasses within the star

7. She's probably the most enjoyable character in the OES degree

8. It is the Covenant of Adoption

11. Her badge is the dove within the star

14. Her duty is to record the good deeds of her companions

15. This NT book is opened in the O.E.S. Degree

17. It represents the Trinity and is part of Martha's sign

18. One of our primary duties in the order is to...

20. This is the pass for ladies in the Q of the S degree

21. It's the secret word upon the block of the star

Name: _____ Date: _____

OES Crossword

Across

1. Name the heroine of the Sister's degree.

3. What is the emblem for Esther

4. What is the mission of the OES?

6. What is the triangle a symbol of?

10. Name of the heroine for the Daughter's degree.

11. What is the theory of the OES founded on?

13. Number of floral emblems

14. In which direction are you traveling

15. The symbol for suffering.

17. A figure having five straight lines.

18. The sacred light of a Eastern Star

19. What is the meaning of the word "Cabalistic"?

Down

2. Make up the central points of the Star.

5. Name of the heroine for the Mother's degree

7. Badge of the Worthy Matron

8. How many are necessary to confer the degrees?

9. What is the least number necessary to organize a Chapter?

12. The key which unlocks the door of a Chapter for a candidate.

16. The emblem for Adah.

ORDER OF THE EASTERN STAR

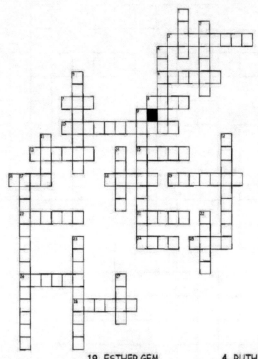

Across
3. ADAH GEM
6. RUTH STATION
7. ESTHER CHRIST SYMBOL
8. ESTHER FLOWER
10. RUTH EMNLEM
13. RUTH SEASON
15. RUTH DEGREE
16. ADAH'S COLOR
18. ADAH STATION

19. ESTHER GEM
20. RUTH COLOR
21. RUTH GEM
24. FRIEND
25. ESTHER DEGREE
26. STAR
28. ADAH FLOWER

Down
1. JUDGES 11:35
2. ADAH SEASON

4. RUTH FLOWER
5. ADAH DEGREE
9. ESTHER EMBLEM
11. MATTHEW 5:8
12. ADAH CHRIST SYMBOL
14. ESTHER STATION
17. RUTH CHRIST SYMBOL
22. ESTHER COLOR
23. ADAH EMBLEM
27. MATTHEW 5:5

Word Bank

ADAH	BLUE	FIRST	DAUGHTER	SWORDVEIL
VIOLET	SAPPHIRE	SPRING	OPEN BIBLE	PURE
RUTH	SECOND	YELLOW	WIDOW	WHEATBARLEY
JASMINE	TOPAZ	SUMMER	LILYOFTHEVALLEY	MEEK
ESTHER	THIRD	WHITE	WIFE	CROWNSEPTER
LILY	DIAMOND	SUN		

OES MATCHING

1. ESTHER SEASON	A. RUBY
2. MATTHEW 5:9	B. FIFTH
3. JOHN 11:26	C. ROSE
4. MARTHA STATION	D. AUTUMN
5. MARTHA COLOR	E. PERSECUTED RIGHTOUENESS SAKE
6. MARTHA DEGREE	F. INTERCHANGEABLE
7. MARTHA EMBLEM	G. SISTER
8. MARTHA FLOWER	H. LION
9. MARTHA GEM	I. FOURTH
10. MARTHA SEASON	J. MOURN
11. MARTHA CHRIST SYMBOL	K. MOTHER
12. MATTHEW 5:4	L. GREEN
13. 2ND JOHN 1:5	M. PEACEMAKERS
14. ELECTA STATION	N. FERN
15. ELECTA COLOR	O. LAMB & CROSS
16. ELECTA DEGREE	P. BROKEN COLUMN
17. ELECTA EMBLEM	Q. RED
18. ELECTA FLOWER	R. MARTHA
19. ELECTA GEM	S. WINTER
20. ELECTA SEASON	T. ELECTA
21. ELECTA CHRIST SYMBOL	U. EMERALD
22. MATTHEW 5:10	V. CUP

Name: _____

OES - STARS

Across
3. II John 1:5
5. Adah's PASS
6. Esther's PASS
8. Electa's PASS
10. Martha's PASS

Down
1. St John 11th Chapter
2. Crown and Scepter
4. Ruth's PASS
7. Judges 11:29-40
9. Sheaf of Barley

192

Notes

notes

notes

_____
_____
_____
_____
_____
_____
_____
_____
_____
_____
_____
_____
_____
_____
_____
_____
_____
_____
_____
_____
_____
_____
_____

notes

notes

notes

notes

notes

notes